Yours Forever

Robbie Dorman

Yours Forever by Robbie Dorman

© 2024 Robert Dorman. All rights reserved.

www.robbiedorman.com

ISBN-13: 978-1-958768-20-4

Cover art by Alex Eckman-Lawn

This is a work of fiction. All characters and events portrayed in this book are fictitious and any resemblance to real people or events is purely coincidental.

No part of this book may be reproduced, stored in a retrieval system, or transmitted in any form or by any means, including mechanical, electric, photocopying, recording, or otherwise, without the prior written permission of the publisher.

For Carrie.

1

Dearest Beloved,

I promise I will return to you.

The travel has been arduous. I have twice now had to change trains because of mechanical issues, the cars slowing, limping, the great machines trodding along their metal feet to the next station, and all of us fleas riding on their backs, disembarking, jumping off at the nearest stop, in some misbegotten town in forgotten America, waiting among the rabble, until a new train can be brought forth, a fresh beast summoned, and then we continue, the ticks and parasites settling into the folds of our raw transport.

Perhaps I am being dramatic, no, I know I am, my misery palpable. I had hoped to get to the House quickly, a three days journey, I was told, but with the delays it will be nearly a week, too long a time. I am already off schedule, and I have mentally shifted my plans, once, twice, and now, if there is another delay, I will have to abandon them all together, and improvise.

And if it was just the mechanical difficulties, I could make due, I would bite my tongue and turn the complaints inward, but no, it was not just the train itself, but the people.

The damnable people.

I had purchased a private room, a worthwhile expense, to give me time to study and sit in quiet. I would venture out for food and drinks, and mingle with the common folk if the need required, but then I could retreat, back into my solitude, where I could read, and sleep, and plan.

But the room was not private, there were no truly private rooms on the train, despite my desperate pleas to the company man, he insisted I must share the cabin, I could not purchase the whole space for myself, the second bed had been sold, I must share it.

Share it with William Boldy, who insisted I call him Billy, and would not leave me alone for a moment, not even a few minutes of study before he intruded, begging for conversation with his moving tongue.

"Where you from, mister?" he asked. He half-sat on the other side of the room, one leg tucked against him, pulled tight. He ate a banana, half peeled, the skin dangling against his hand, browning. The form of the fruit wetly clung to his gums as he spoke, and I saw the dirt underneath his fingertips, and the yellow, white-brown meat stuck to his teeth.

"New England," I spoke, hoping the broad answer would satisfy.

"Boston?"

"Near," I said. I would not give this man information he hadn't earned. It was worth more than him.

"Spent some time up there," he said, chewing on the banana, more meat in his mouth, mashing. "It's a nice place, it is. I worked in the yard at a factory, on the north side, and it paid well enough, but the foreman, he was a real ass, and wouldn't put me through, no matter how I worked, and—"

He continued, Billy did, and my eyes considered him as he prattled, but I only saw the teeth move, as he chewed and spat out the dribble about his life, about his work, about what brought him to middle America, about the American Dream, and I could not listen. I considered him, and he spoke, but my mind went elsewhere.

My mind went to you.

My solace. As you have been. Ever since we found each other, you have been my retreat.

As he spoke, I focused on you instead, a balm, and his words faded into the background. Eventually he went to drink, and left me in quiet, and I could study again.

Perhaps it was foolish to bring all the works, but I did not know what I would need once I arrived, what reference I would require, and so I brought them all. Yes, the books are heavy, but it is worth the struggle to have them at the ready. And despite that I have read them all, and notated them, I still find additional details. Fresh perspective and knowledge.

As I near the House, the proximity to the banal masses and the filth of society becomes more tolerable. Perhaps it is because I draw closer to my goal, and closer to returning to you, returning to you victorious. And truly, any punishment, any sacrifice is worthwhile. Stepping foot in the city, into the train station, made my skin crawl. But I kept my thoughts on you, my faith in your love, and I persisted, and now, now, I am closer than I have ever been to my life's work.

Billy returned in the middle of my study and asked intrusive questions about the nature of the book I read. It was Van der Graaf's work, which I find reliable, despite that it is half unreadable, written in a code which I cannot break or parse.

He was sloppy, his lips wet, his gaped eyes staring at me, and then at the book I read, even as night fell, but I rebuked him, keeping him from the knowledge contained within. He hadn't earned access, of course he hadn't, he had given no part of himself to you, hadn't dedicated, hadn't kept his faith, and so I denied him, shutting the tome closed.

William stared at me with a devilish gaze, his workman eyes, with dark bags underneath, with sooted fingernails, and deep anxiety rose in me, that he would fight me for my denial, that he would raise his lunchbox fists, but instead he sank back, exhaustion overtaking him. Without another word to me, he laid back and closed his eyes, and promptly fell asleep.

My heart eased. I did not want to fight him. He was a brute and surely had me outmatched in strength and endurance. My intelligence would do me no good in a fistfight.

But he slumbered and left me alone with my studies. The train moved through the evening and into the night. Through the darkness, it cut closer to the House, and to your heart.

I grow tired. This train shall arrive tomorrow and I will see the House. And as much as my stomach tenses at the thought, it is a blessing. It is an opportunity one does not see in a thousand years.

Mark my words, I will return to you victorious. I will save you. My faith will drive me forward, ever forward.

I will find your heart.

Yours Forever,

Henry Collingsworth

2

Dearest,

    The accursed train journey is finally over. I arrived at Plainmoor station this morning, the final engine being sound enough to carry me the rest of the way. I was the only one who disembarked here, thankfully enough.

    William wished me well on my trip, the smell of stale vodka still on his breath, and I smiled at him as best I could, the smile all the easier because I would be rid of him forever, and on my way.

    But mayhap I should have counted my blessings with my drunken roommate, because despite his crawling skin and dirty hands, he meant me no ill well, despite my disgust with him.

    The residents of Plainmoor were different.

    Different, in that they were open with their hatred of me. The train station was mostly empty, but the few people there all stared at me with open loathing as I moved through the station, and the baggage man looked at me with contempt as he wheeled my luggage, to where my driver would pick me up.

    I left him an overlarge tip, but it did nothing to ease the antipathy in his gaze. He left me for my driver, who was punctual.

    His punctuality is the only thing I can commend. He did not disguise his disdain for me. Venom poured from his eyes as he got out of the car, and put my bags in the trunk, and then opened the door for me, following the rote rules of order and decorum, spite emanating from his pores.

I got into the car, and he slid behind the wheel, looking at me in the mirror, before starting the engine and cruising away.

I sat in the backseat. The car was nice, well-kept, and smelled of flowers. But I felt the bitter hatred from the driver, felt the anger rising off him, hitting me in waves. I wanted to say nothing. To ignore him for my short drive out to the House, but I realized I couldn't sit in ignorance. Knowledge is valuable, and the residents of Plainmoor may be of assistance in that regard.

"Excuse me, sir," I said, and his hateful eyes rested on me again.

"Yes?"

"Am I wrong to say that I feel some resentment from you, and the other people in town, toward myself?"

His eyes considered me. His nose rankled.

"Resentment," he said. He breathed smoke. "I don't know what you mean."

"Please, speak plainly, sir. It will not impact your pay."

He considered me, then. He stared straight ahead again, as the car drove past empty fields and abandoned homes. I had read that Plainmoor was a farming town. A trading town. But I saw no farms. No trucks. The railway wasn't active.

"We didn't want the Suffolk house built," he said, finally. He paused. "We never did. You've bought the house, correct?"

"Yes," I said. There was no use in lying to the man.

"What are your plans for it?"

"I have none, as of yet. I've yet to visit."

He stared at me again, and I saw the first glimpse of an emotion other than anger.

"He brought something here."

"Excuse me?" I asked. We passed more empty fields, once sown and harvested, now barren.

"Not ten years ago—the town was prosperous. The ground here is good. We've never seen drought, or famine. The people work hard, and the train station was built. We thought it would bring even more money to the area. Help us build more. Instead, it brought us James Suffolk."

The Architect. They had no love for him, either.

"I'm not familiar with the man," I said. I would lie, now.

"He built the house you bought," said the driver. "He bought the land, the empty plot in the middle of that wild forest, and he built that mansion, and then he vanished."

"I knew he went missing," I said. "And his loan defaulted, and the bank sold the house to me."

"We tried to buy it," said the driver. He took a deep breath. "I apologize for the hatefulness. I do. But the town wanted the house."

"Why?"

"Because he brought something here, Mr. Collingsworth."

His stare was cold and direct as they drove down the gravel road.

"What did he bring?"

"We don't know," he said. "But it's in that house. He built the house, and he moved in, and since that day, the town has seen nothing but wreck and heartache. The fields have gone barren. The crops that have grown have been filled with rot. Children have been born deaf and dumb. Cancers have eaten at us. Businesses have gone under, and everyone with the means has fled the town. Whether it be the house itself, or something contained within—it has cursed us."

I said nothing.

He stared at me. "Please, Mr. Collingsworth. The house, or whatever is in it—destroy it."

By that point, we had arrived at the gates to the Suffolk House, wrought iron, attached to a fence that enclosed the property. The iron rose into the sky above us, into fierce spikes. The driver got out and pushed open the gate, the metal hinges creaking with disuse. My ears ached as the sharp sound echoed through the quiet.

He got back in and finished our drive down the long gravel driveway. The rocks clattered and rattled under the car, and the driver slowed to a crawl. The property had never been cleared, deep woods on each side of the path, threatening to move in and cut off access, the trees soaring above us, cutting off all light. Indeed, although it was mid-morning, it felt like late evening. The sun set early on the Suffolk House.

And then I saw it.

The House.

The canopy vanished and the sun pierced through, highlighting the House. It stood three stories tall, expansive, stretching over a hundred feet to the left and right, east and west. It was painted white, or had been. But the paint had faded, and the sun, despite shining down on it, seemed dim. The House was dirty, yes, with some vines and foliage growing up, and around it, but the more I looked at it, the darker and dingier it felt.

The House was a plantation style home, with massive columns dominating the front of the building, with sweeping porches covering the exterior. Gabled windows stood at the top of the third story, but I could not see within. All the windows had shutters, and all were closed.

The eyes of the House were shut, blinded, kept only to the darkness.

There was no furniture on the porch. No rocking chair, no small table to set a drink upon on a quiet evening. I pondered if Suffolk had ever lived in this House? Or had it always been a prison to him?

The House loomed over us, and the driver refused to look, his eyes staying on the gravel, on the steering wheel, on his hands.

The driveway circled next to the front of the home, and as we came to a stop, I got out immediately, standing next to the car. I had to see it with my bare eyes, with no glass in between. I had to be sure.

I stood, and I took in the House, and I knew then. I knew your heart was contained within.

Certainly, the driver's account of the sudden curse upon the town corroborated everything. About the Architect, and the records left by him and his associates. About the path he tread, which I retraced, following him to Plainmoor, and to this House.

But still, words on a page, and lines on a map, are no excuse for the feeling of faith invigorated. Of the deep connection of love and adoration. And despite everything, there had been doubt within me.

Doubt the purchase of the home had been foolhardy. That my parents, and their criticism, father's steadfast complaints about my pursuit, my "obsession" as he had called it, and my mother, and her nagging clucks, that both had been right. That I should have listened.

That I should have forgotten you.

I hated it, hated the voice that lingered in my mind, but that hatred did not dispel the fact it persisted, that I had wasted my time and money and my love on this foolish quest.

But Beloved, I swear, when I set my eyes on the House this morning—that doubt was dispelled.

Because I felt you, deep inside. My heart thumped in my chest, rattling

Yours Forever

against my ribs, against my lungs, the profound ache I could not push away easing, disappearing.

Vanishing, because I felt your heart beat alongside mine.

Yours Forever,

Henry

3

The driver wouldn't follow me inside. All the anger, all the rage, had disappeared from him, replaced only by his fear, and he helped lift my luggage from the car, but begged me to allow him not to enter.

I gave my permission, and he drove away, leaving me alone with the House.

Alone with you.

But not only with you. Because despite your heart beating somewhere deep inside, I felt something else. A presence, something alien, unkind, untoward.

And just like I knew your heart was here, somewhere, I knew he was here, somewhere. I sensed him, the same anger and outrage that the driver had felt, the people of the town, but now as an oppression, an atmosphere of disgust that permeated every surface of the home.

The Architect was here.

Because of course he was. He had designed the home, had built it, and had gone to extraordinary lengths to hide your heart inside. He had curated everything in this place, had inhabited the House the entire time. Of course he would be here.

But was he alive?

It was a question I had pondered for much longer than today, Beloved, but one I had let linger in the back of my mind, because it was a question unanswerable, not until I was here, until I fully mapped the grounds, to search the entire structure.

He couldn't be alive. No one had seen him in years, not since he had completed building the House, disappeared inside, and never emerged again.

Months had passed, and a groundskeeper had gone looking for him and found nothing. An empty house. More time passed, and more people had come. Auditors from the government, pursuing their taxes, and people from Plainmoor, seeking cause for their cancers.

But they found nothing, and the county seized the property, perhaps urged by the same residents, who wanted it, to demolish the home and forever bury your heart in its wreckage.

He couldn't be alive. If he was, he would do everything in his power to hold this House, to conceal it. To make it an impregnable fortress, to hold you eternally. His disappearance is not in the best interest of his intended mission, and therefore, the only remaining explanation is his untimely death.

But that raises the question—where is his body?

They searched the House thoroughly. I know they did, and there was no helping it. But they did not find his corpse, not hide nor hair, neither any smell of cadaverous origin.

And they didn't find your heart, that much is clear.

They found nothing.

And despite my logic and rationale, there is another explanation to the location of the Architect.

That he is still here, in a hiding place known only to him, and he waits there, waiting for me, knowing I would come, knowing I would come desperately searching, and then he would spring his trap. He would wait until my back was turned, until I slept, or until I was fingertips away from your heart, and then he would strike me down, another victim of his dark quest.

And Suffolk would wait in the shadows. His pernicious intelligence was abundant, and underestimating him, or casting away the thought of a trap as ludicrous, would only bring my downfall. Your heart serves as ample lure.

I felt him there, as I took in the House, waiting, listening. There was no sound, the space filled with utter silence. I stood in the grand foyer and waited. No creaking stairs from above, no distant, muffled noises. Nothing. The House was silent.

It smelled like the grave. Of dirt, of a funeral, of the end of things. I desperately pushed the air from my nostrils, trying to rid myself of the smell, but the scent permeated the House, and as I moved, leaving my luggage behind, the odor followed.

I wandered into the central chamber of the home, the large open area, a lounge of sorts, a fireplace dominating the space, but it was a meeting place, a place where the various hallways and staircases of the home all intersected, stairs up to the second and third floors, and long halls spanning to the east and west and north, leading off to the wings of the home.

The gravedirt followed me, inhabiting my nostrils, and I peered down the west and east hallways, and saw the great double doors on each side, toward the wings. I stared to the north, and only a single door led to the north wing, and an idea germinated inside the fertility of my mind, but I waited. It would take time to bloom, and so I gave it room to grow.

I pushed away the thoughts of the Architect, and of the smell, and of the silence. I returned to my reason. To you.

Your heart is somewhere inside this place, and I will find it.

But to do that, I must comb the House. Dig through Suffolk's secrets. I will find a temporary bed, and I will plan. Until morrow.

Yours Forever

4

I slept uneasily last night.

I slept in a bed here, one bed of the Architect. There are many beds in the House, I've come to discover. Many bedrooms. Most were unoccupied, the beds never slept in. I took a bedroom in the center of the House, and barricaded the door before I slept.

The House was silent, and there was no intrusion. I still felt his presence, enough to unsettle me.

But I found sleep in thoughts of your heart.

I explored the House today. I woke up early and ate some provisions I had brought. I ate quickly, sitting at a small table in the center of the House's hub, the middle of the three spokes: west, east, north.

I know I should have tempered my expectations, but I had hoped. I had hoped I would find you quickly. Despite the House's mammoth size, I had dreamed I would locate you within a day or two, and then be on my way, leaving the House to wreck and ruin, letting it and the Architect sink into the earth.

But I was foolish to think so, foolish to think the auditors had done a hasty job when they themselves had explored. I was provided blueprints of the House, along with a rough layout of the rooms when I purchased the deed.

The auditors were thorough. I went room by room, making notes. I consult them now, and yes, everything was where they noted.

The west wing first.

Thirteen bedrooms, three of which were master suites, one on each floor, ground, second, third. The third floor master suite has the massive gabled window that overlooks the front of the grounds. Each of the suites also has an in suite bathroom. There are six other bathrooms, marking nine total in the west wing.

I scoured each of the rooms, but there was very little to survey. They are furnished, surely, with a bed, a vanity, a desk, a night table, a bookshelf. All lovely furniture, handmade, made by the Architect himself. After finding his mark on a chair, I located it on every piece of furniture. Even with my distaste for the man, I must respect the toil required to fill a mansion with his woodworking. Hours of sweat at the saw, to conjoin wood and make dozens of tables and chairs and beds. This was his life.

Beyond the fixtures, there was little else to discover. No belongings. No history. The living spaces had not been lived in. A guest wing for guests that never came. Was this place ever intended for life?

I walked the spaces with intention, listening to the walls, to the floors, but there was nothing hidden. The blueprints and layouts matched. The auditors had no prejudice. They wrote what they found, and every room agreed with their findings.

The west wing took until lunchtime, as I marked each room as I searched, compiling my notes, confirming the conclusions of the auditors. I ate more of my provisions, reading over my findings. I looked over my notes, sitting in one of the Suffolk's chairs, eating from his table, looking for anything, any sign of something hidden, or obtrusive, or strange.

But there was nothing. My findings agreed with the auditors. You are not in the west wing.

After checking my notes, I moved to the east.

I looked at the blueprints, and I conferred with the auditor's findings as well, before I searched. I came to a conclusion quickly. The auditors had come to the same conclusion. They did their due diligence. They were professionals, without bias.

As am I, and I went room by room in the east, as I did the west.

Thirteen bedrooms.

Three master suites, with in suite bathrooms.

Nine total bathrooms.
Each bedroom furnished.
A bed.
A vanity.
A desk.
A night table.
A bookshelf.
All bearing Suffolk's mark.

I walked each foot of the wing, the living spaces, the bed and bathrooms. I sat in the chairs and listened to the floors and walls. They hold no secrets.

It could not tell a lie, just as honest as its twin.

Indeed, the west and east are the same, mirrored. The auditors realized quickly the Architect built them to the same specifications. The rooms, the walls, the floors, the layout, the furniture—all the same.

I took notes, as I did the west, being sure to note anything of importance. I assessed, knocking on the walls, looking for anything that didn't measure up. A lost foot, or a loose floorboard, anywhere where he could have hidden you, out of sight, an unobtrusive spot possibly overlooked.

But the math is sound. Not a foot of wood or beam misplaced. No place to hide. The Architect was true to his title.

The east took nearly the full afternoon, as I double checked my math, and double backed to my notes on the west.

I ate dinner, the same provisions I had brought from home. They would last me for days still, but doubt has grown in me. This food will not last me my entire stay.

But I ate, and then I stood in the hub again, the center of the House, and looked to the west, and to the east, and saw the double doors that led to each wing, down the long corridors that led to them.

Mirrors of each other. The same, down to the inch, measured and placed with utmost care.

Then I looked to the north. A single door led there, and the idea that had sprung forth the day prior was given full bloom. The north was where you were kept. The east, the west—they were distractions. The north wing is where I will find you.

5

I explored the north wing, and I found evidence of the Architect.

The north is separate from the east and west. Separate in all ways, I discovered. Different entirely. The layout is unique, bearing no resemblance to the mirror twins of the east and west.

There are thirteen bedrooms in the north, thirteen bathrooms. Thirteen of everything worth counting. It is a pattern born out by the auditors. There was no speculation in their counting, only the bare facts, but I can imagine the thoughts of the men who visited here, who came to follow the trail of the missing James Suffolk. Of the twin west and east wings, and then of the north, which bore multiple instances of the unlucky number thirteen.

The number came up in my studies occasionally, but perhaps Suffolk made a connection I did not. I will have to study.

But I did my due diligence, just as I did in the east and west. I counted the rooms, and walked them, step by step. I measured, and knocked, and listened to the walls and floors.

The furniture bore his mark, just as it did in the other wings, with precise measure and craft. But these chairs, the beds, the desks and vanities, they were not the same. They each bore unique designs.

The master bed in particular. The outer side of the footboard is engraved with thirteen points of light. Each an eight-point star. Thirteen stars. Each emblazoned with starfire in the dark tone of the wood. It is singular among everything. I probed the engraving, each of the points an indentation. But nothing came of it. Is it special?

If there was intent, I do not see it, not yet. Did the Architect grow bored? Or is this build important, a purpose I cannot see?

But as I explored the north wing, I saw more than just the fair measure of the room, of the wing, of the tables and chairs.

I saw the measure of the Architect himself, because his possessions are interned here. And not just a few, but many. Perhaps all, perhaps all of his worldly belongings, the things he valued above all else, all still kept in the House.

I understood the purchase conferred everything contained within the House, and the auditors were thorough, of course they were, I've made note of it several times. They counted the furniture, and communicated to me extensively how many beds I would receive, how many tables and chairs, the number of rugs, and paintings, and vases. Of those, I was quite prepared.

But in the long inventory of times included with the purchase of the House, the Architect's belongings were all contained within a single line item.

Personal effects of the past owner.

The auditors thought it most effective to simply include them with the sale of the home. Suffolk had no inheritors. If the new owner wished to dispose of his belongings, it was up to them.

My research of Suffolk found little of his personal history. Even with the work of a private detective, nothing was found of him, aside from his work in academia, and then his jaunt to this House. If not for my own research, I would not know of his pursuit of your heart, and of its secreting inside the home.

Suffolk had buried his past, much like your heart.

But now, some of it has been laid bare.

And I realize I may need to become intimate with it, if I wish to progress, as understanding the Architect may be the key to getting to you.

That one simple line item, personal effects of the past owner, I will expand and make my own list. Room by room, I noted where the items lay, and then I collected them, and assembled them all, into one collection. An entire life, laid bare in front of me.

Hundreds of items. Keepsakes, photographs, albums, collections and pieces of his life. If I did not despise the man as a nemesis, these items would attach myself to him, would extend a tether between us, connect us, but I would not and did not allow it. Regardless of the history of the man, his sin against you is too great to forgive.

I assemble his life.

Photographs of him as a young man. A boy, really. Dressed in clothes that betray a rough upbringing. A father and mother, and then just a father. A jump in time, and then college, and a life in academia.

I watch Suffolk age and grow, and there are women. And then only one woman. And I see Suffolk smile.

And then there is a child. The child grows, as does Suffolk and his wife. They age together.

But then, there is only Suffolk. His smile has vanished. The photos are rote, a marker, a measure of his age and placement. Suffolk continues to age, but the child and wife stay frozen in time, the last marker those photographs.

I found these photos in what must be Suffolk's bedroom, central to the north wing, in the thirteenth bedroom, right in the middle. The things he treasured most. The photos he saw as he fell asleep, and as he woke from slumber.

With all my research, as I tracked his movement and his study. As I followed him across the globe, to the place of your sleeping heart, where he stole it in the dead of night, under your eyes and ears, and absconded with the most priceless item in the world, and then returned to this House. I found almost nothing from the man himself. Always third-hand accounts, signs of what he studied, and what he read. Eyewitnesses, friends, associates. The people who knew him, who swam in his wake, the great shark.

But the man left no notes, no work.

With these photographs, with these keepsakes, I have begun to piece it together. Born of low station, raised by a father. An academic who found love, who had a child. Who lost both.

Why did he pursue you? Why did he steal? And why did he hide it, so deep, in this House?

More secrets. I will need to study.

6

I have spent days exploring the north wing and Suffolk's belongings, but I am no closer to your heart.

The north wing holds secrets. That much is apparent, but how to expose them is not. I have pored over his possessions, but there are no details of the House, or of your heart. He kept no notes of the building of the House, or anything after the theft of you.

There are old novels with flowers pressed between the pages, inscribed with small scribblings, an ink pen underlining passages, ascribing minor questions in the margins. I presume the work of his late wife, but there is no way of knowing.

The childish drawings are easier to source, but other than the sentimental value to Suffolk, they provide no clues to the home of your heart.

I looked over every one before placing it with all the other items, ultimately useless to anyone but the Architect himself.

Old belongings of his wife and child, but almost nothing from him. And no books, no research, no work. No evidence of his toil on the House, of the building. Of the making of the furniture, of the walls and floors and planning and thousands of hours of effort that went into making this prison and doubt weighs on my mind because he has sealed your tomb well, and I have yet to find a crack in which I can insert my fingers and pull.

How did he build this place, and where does it hide you?

I measured, over and over, the thirteen bedrooms, and the thirteen bathrooms, and the living spaces, thirteen in total, and the north wing in its entirety, and there are no discrepancies. No space where the measurements do not add up, no obvious place to hide. No, the auditors would have discovered it, and they found nothing out of the ordinary, no, nothing aside from the missing man, and the House that carries an onerous curse, sold to a gentleman from out of town, looking for the heart of his destined love.

It is enough to drive me mad. I have chased Suffolk across the country at great personal expense, and although I am now closer than I have ever been, I still feel like a wide chasm exists between me and you, and that is what truly pains me. That ocean between us, one I must bridge with my intellect and intelligence. I must defeat the planning of Suffolk, who had the benefit of cunning and stealth, moving in the dark.

I finally removed myself from the north and went back to the central hub, back to my luggage, and my primitive base camp. I had yet to unpack all my things, only taking what I required when I needed it. I again looked at the layout of the House provided by the auditors, and at the blueprints given.

The blueprints were not originals, not the work of Suffolk. They were created by an engineer after the fact, alongside the work of the auditors. If there was something secret laid inside the walls and ceilings, these blueprints wouldn't provide it. But they seemed sound, the auditors hiring a competent man who did reliable work. The measurements were accurate.

I stared at them until my eyes hurt, then stopped. I was waiting for a secret to leap from the pages, and it simply would not happen.

I paused to eat. My sundries were running at an end. I would have to return to town soon enough and stock up. I would have to use the kitchen in the House as well, despite my resistance to using anything Suffolk had built. It was a useless urge on my part. I was reliant on the man, and there was no way around it. To resist it would only slow me down and make my work harder still. I already slept in a bed of his making—

I stopped then, something clicking into place in my mind.

His bedroom, the thirteenth bedroom in the north, in the middle of the wing.

The west and east, mirror twins of each other.

I peered at the layout, stepping back, looking at it in whole. My eyes scanned it. I saw the symmetry. How did I not see it sooner? I was too absorbed in the photos and keepsakes, obsessing over minor details of the Architect's life, of some personal tragedy or reasoning. The motive did not matter.

The layout had been sketched on multiple pieces of paper, and I cobbled them together, and then I folded them over, so the west and east wings were overlaid each other. Both the hub and the north wing were cut in half, laying over on each other, and my thought was proved true. The north wing cut in half mirrored itself, and the bedroom in the middle was Suffolk's own room, and in the center of the room laid his bed, split right in half.

I left behind my sundries and the layout, and walked straight to his bedroom, where I had collected the keepsakes and photographs. I went to the bed, and stopped, staring at it.

It was a common bed, a queen sized bed, large for one man. I had looked below the bed; I had looked below every bed, and there was nothing hiding beneath, nothing in the floorboards, at least nothing obvious. But I was beyond the obvious, and I grabbed at the corner of the bed frame and dragged. I would reveal the floor beneath it, and see if there was something hiding. But the bed would not move.

I tried again, pulling hard, but it would not budge, and it was not a matter of strength. I am not the strongest man, but this bed would not shift if pulled by Hercules himself.

I examined the four corners of the bed, and the head and footboards, but their connection to the floor seemed normal. No extraneous bolts, no screws, or nails, or glues of any kind.

My heart thudded. I was close now. I took a deep breath.

I stared at the bed. It had been made and never unmade, perhaps by the Architect himself. The sheets were white and clean, the comforter a simple thick brown blanket that would keep the chill out most winter nights. Looking at it, it was innocuous, just a bed.

It struck me, then.

I must use the home as a home. I must use the kitchen, and live in the Suffolk House.

I must sleep in his bed before I can reveal its secret.

Tonight, I sleep as Suffolk slept.

7

I slept as Suffolk slept, and I was right. It was the key to everything.

I moved my belongings into his bedroom. I wanted them close. I studied my notes, and my old research, while night fell, and the House grew dark. The House has electricity, but I kept a lantern burning instead of relying on the circuits.

It had been a long day, and I grew tired, and yawns continued to interrupt my studying, but I resisted, sitting at Suffolk's desk, his bed standing behind me.

I didn't want to sleep in it. As strange as it may sound, I worried his spirit would possess me in the night. The photos, the keepsakes—the presence I felt when I first arrived—it was there, almost tangible, in the air. And no matter how much of his belongings I moved, it was still there, sticking to me.

The bed loomed behind me, but I felt my eyelids droop as I tried to read over one of your books, and I knew if I would sleep in the bed, I would need to do it now, while I had the energy to mount it.

I stood, and blowing out the lantern, I pulled aside the thick brown blanket and white sheet underneath, and crawled into the bed. The mattress was soft, royal.

I laid down, pulling the sheet and blanket over me. I settled into the dark.

I had slept in the House for almost a week now, and had grown accustomed to the creaks and settling of the place, like any home would have, especially one still new to the Earth, especially one of this size, which flexed and moved with its great weight.

But I could not help but focus on the noises. As I laid in Suffolk's bed, I felt his creation around me, prison and home. The wood squeaked and squealed, shuddered and moaned, and in the dark of the House I imagined it squeezing in on me. I felt it shift, and squall, and my chest shook, and I couldn't catch my breath, no matter how much I panted, like a tired dog, my tongue greedily lapping at the air.

But I wouldn't turn on the light, I wouldn't, I refused. The Architect would not win this battle, and neither would the House. Somehow I knew that to turn on the light was failure, a cowardly retreat to my lantern I would not suffer. I had traveled so far and had incurred great expense. The willowy sounds of lumber and beam would not defeat me.

I stopped, and stared out into the darkness of the bedroom, and took deep breaths, controlling my breathing. The House's sounds were just that, just sounds, and I focused instead on the bed, and my breaths, and soon the aural cacophony surrounding me died down, if it was ever there at all, only a part of my imagining.

I thought of you, and of your heart, residing somewhere within this great House, and reached out to it, feeling for it with my mind. Dreaming of the heartbeat that would match mine one day. I would emerge from the home with your heart, in triumph, and defeat the Architect, and his machinations that have extended beyond his death, if death truly had captured him.

But even with the sounds quelled, I could not sleep, despite my exhaustion. I tossed and turned, trying to find a desperate comfort, but every movement only made it worse. I rolled to my left side, and then to my right, and every time a tension rolled through my back. I laid flat and hoped it would bring me sleep. But no matter how little I moved, I felt the pressure in my spine. And then I realized.

I forgot my earlier proclamation, tossing it aside, and jumped out of bed, reaching for my lantern. I lit it quickly and cast the darkness from the room. It was as I left it in the light, no difference, no ghostly forces filling the space. I would need light to see. See the first of Suffolk's secrets.

The pillows and blankets were cover, camouflage, a smokescreen, and I threw them aside, and then grabbed my pocket knife, unsheathing the three-inch blade, and sliding it into the mattress, disemboweling the down filled fabric. It ripped and teared as I pulled, and then I threw the knife aside, the blade embedded in the floor, my hands seizing at the edges of the new orifice and pulling it open, down spilling out into the air. I tore at it, throwing it behind me, and then I found it, unearthing the source of my frustration. But also, the key to your heart.

Inside the mattress, the wooden piece. Thin, long, made of the same wood as the bed, as all the furniture. A shape at the end. An eight-point star.

Of course.

I pulled it from its hiding place, and went to the footboard, brightened by my lantern, flickering light showing the thirteen points. The shapes matched, the wooden piece, the engraving. But which of the thirteen?

I studied them. Are you one of them, Beloved?

If you are, you are the central. The most important. The largest.

One of the thirteen points was lower than the others, central, the largest, dominating. I slid the wooden piece home.

The bed broke, sliding in half with a great crack, the mattress pushed aside, two halves of the bed rotating, and then sliding down into the floor. Because it was not only the bed that had broken open, but the floor itself, beneath the bed, a great and perfect line opening in the boards, rotating up and sliding into a recess like the bed itself.

I stood back and stared. The floor opened in front of my eyes, and I held the lantern up to see clearly. As the floor opened, a great crevice became visible.

It was impossible. I had measured every inch of Suffolk's House, and every single piece was accounted for. There was no room for this hole, and yet, there it was.

As the floor and bed stopped, now completely gone, a deep stairwell declined in front of me, down into the depths of the north wing. A stairwell that could not exist, stairs that defied physics and architecture.

The bed had been a key, and below it lay a passage, down into the depths. Surely, your heart was down below, and Suffolk had slept over it, guarding it in his sleep.

And now, now I must delve.

8

I should have prepared. I should have regrouped, and planned a more cautious expedition. But I saw the downward stairs, and a great curiosity seized me, a true feeling of the unknown taking a hold of me. How could it not? I had embarked on this perilous journey, crossing thousands of miles at great personal cost, and this was progress. A downward staircase, the stairs descending into darkness.

Your heart lay down those stairs.

And there was time, with the whole of the day to explore. I would not throw away the opportunity. Or delay it any longer. I had waited years for this. I went down, bringing a lantern and my day kit, a simple pouch with the essentials I always carried. A compass, a pocket knife, a box of matches, and other various minor items of utility. But it was all I brought. I did not know what I would find.

The light from the House only traveled a short distance, before it died out, the stairs continuing down into darkness, unseeable, and I held the lantern aloft as I crossed into the shadow, and it revealed only more stairs, and I continued down. I did not count them heading downward, although I should have, but the distance was great, the darkness taking back the ground I had covered, and after long minutes of walking down, I looked back up to see the path dim, too far to see any evidence of the Suffolk

House.

And I was suddenly seized by a sinister terror. Of the passage shutting itself once again. Of being stranded in the shadows, shut inside the House, the trap by the Architect abruptly sprung, trapped in the same tomb as your great organ.

I froze, thinking to charge up the stairs, to sprint away from this snare, perhaps to save myself at the last moment.

But instead I waited, my breath the only sound in the dark, the wooden walls on both sides of me. I paused, holding back my terror. I could not flee at the mere thought of danger.

I waited, and the stairs did not move, and the passageway down did not close. I took in a great breath and let it out slowly, and my heartbeat slowed, and I continued down.

I did not count the stairs on the way down, and I did not clock my travel, but I traveled down for a long time, the moment the stairs stopped a sudden shock, finding myself on level ground again, at a short landing that connected to a hallway, a T junction, leading left and right. A door stood directly in front of me, opposite the landing.

I examined the landing, and I was surprised to see a switch. A light switch, identical to the ones above.

Electricity? Down this far? It was impossible. But my curiosity got the better of me, and I flipped the switch.

Electric lamps kicked on above me, lighting the space.

I peered to the left and right, bulbs spaced every ten feet, giving ample illumination. It made little sense, but if it meant I would not have to carry a lantern, all the better.

I blew it out and put it down beside me on the landing. I considered the door in front of me.

It was a simple wooden door, not dissimilar from the doors in the House, but above it was the same diagram from the bed, where I had inserted the wooden key. But there was no void, no place for a key in this version, instead the thirteen points were empty.

But not all. Four of them were lit, small points of light, the rest dark, devoid.

Four points of thirteen. I could not parse the combination, as I stared at it. The door beckoned to me. Should I open it and find out what lay inside?

My hand went to the knob and tested it. It was unlocked. I peered to the left and right, at the matching hallways that traveled out of sight, wooden floors, again matching the floors of the House.

Had Suffolk laid these floors himself, in this impossible underground? Had he wired the lights?

I let go of the handle, backing away. I would not enter the first door I found. The four points of light of thirteen meant something, I knew, and my caution kept me from entering. Not yet.

Instead, I turned to the right. The hallway led a great distance before it ended, too far to see the details. But I saw many intersections, hallways leading to the right and left. I glanced back in the other direction, and saw something similar, different in distance and minutia, but still other parallel, joining hallways.

I looked again, straight ahead, and saw it was not just bare hallway, but other doors, matching the door behind me.

A challenge of navigation it would be. Had the Architect constructed a maze?

Does your heart lie at the center?

Well, if this is a maze, then I must simply my find my way to that center. A simple matter.

Or so I thought. I chose right, the decision arbitrary, and I am right-handed, so I followed nature. I would make only right turns, and with enough time, I would find myself in the center of the maze.

I would find myself at your heart.

I passed a door on my left, and I stopped to study it. Or more accurately, to study the same thirteen stars above it. Indeed, it was the same engraving, as the bed, as the first door I encountered, with thirteen points, but the same four were not lit as the first door. Indeed, there were seven now, only one similar from the first engraving. Seven points of light, a different orientation.

Even so, I would not open any doors, not until I found the center of the maze.

I passed the door, and turned right at the hallway, which matched the previous, but much shorter. I saw the end, and there was another door, this time on my right. I paused again, making note of the engraving. Six stars lit this time, six points of light, another different orientation.

I moved on, the hallway turning to the left, and I continued, turning left, because a left turn is just three rights, and I would find another right, if the maze was true.

And I turned, another hallway, longer than the previous, and I saw three doors, two on the left, one on the right, with multiple branching hallways, but the first turn was to the right and I followed it.

It led to another hallway, and more doors, and here I make note I should have stopped. I should have held caution tight, but no, I thought I understood the breadth of the Architect's plan, and held tight to the laws of physics and chemistry.

I should have known better, but I must also plead the hope to locate you had sprung high in my heart. It urged me on, telling me you would be right around the next bend, that the bounds of the maze couldn't contain me.

It compelled me onward, insisting I had conquered the worst of Suffolk's obstacles, and must merely find my way to the heart of the maze to recover the heart of you.

I will not speak to the finer details of my journey through the maze on this day, because, in all honesty, I cannot recall all of them. I know I stayed true to my pathfinding, of always turning right, of not opening any of the many, many doors I encountered. There was nothing else of note in the environment. Always the same wooden walls, the same hardwood flooring.

I continued on, hurrying. I was sure my plan would lead me to the center of the maze. How could it not? I checked my watch periodically, making note of the time. It seemed to crawl, but felt like a boon. I would find the key to this in record time, and return to the House successfully, and leave this place forever.

But soon I felt the pangs of hunger, a slight growl at first, and then the deep aching pain striking through my stomach. I had eaten a hearty meal before my departure, only a couple of hours prior. I should not be hungry.

I checked the time again, and only minutes had passed since I checked it last. It didn't seem possible. Might my watch be affected by Suffolk's touch as well?

This was when the impossible nature of the place weighed on my mind. Of the sheer size, of the depth in the earth, of the electric lights, of the wooden walls and floors, and of the many doors, all with different orientation of thirteen lights.

Taking one at a time, I could explain away my doubts. But in total, it was clear Suffolk had gone further with his prison. He had delved into magicks, but in a way unfamiliar to me.

This is when I stopped, taking stock. I could not trust my watch. I realized I was more than hungry. I was ravenous. How long had I truly been exploring? How many turns had I made, and how much distance had I traveled?

And now that I had stopped, I listened. I had walked steadfast, at a measured but harried pace, my feet stamping on the wooden boards, the sound bouncing off the walls, my own footsteps and breath in my ears.

But now I had finally stopped, after what was assuredly hours, and I still heard footsteps.

They were distant, soft, but they were there, echoing off the wooden walls and floors, traveling down hall and passageways. But only for a moment, and then they were gone again, and I was left in silence.

I held my breath, the only sound I heard the blood in my ears, but there was nothing else, no more echoing footsteps.

Had I really heard them? I could not trust the passage of time. Could I trust my own senses? Was I being stalked? What creature shared this maze with me?

Was it Suffolk himself?

They entered my mind in a blur, a whirlwind of thoughts, but then a distinct sound pushed them all away.

The sound of a great clock tower.

The sounds of gears turning, of some enormous engine, as metal cranked against metal. The ground itself shook.

A thought leaped to my mind, and I forced myself to move back the way I came. I sprinted as hard and as fast as my legs would allow, panting, my breath hot in my throat. I retraced my steps, only taking lefts now, and the maze shifted behind me. I did not spare a glance backwards, lest I turn to salt.

I had no breath, at the limit of my ability, but I ran regardless, and the ground shifted beneath me and as I neared the end of the hallway, I leaped.

I landed hard on the wooden floors, my ribs and chest aching from the impact. I glanced behind me and saw the floor pivot, the hallway move, rotating, disappearing, and then the space behind was now only the same wooden wall.

I coiled, to push myself up, to sprint from the shifting walls, but then the gears had quieted, and vibration ceased.

Sweat dripped from my forehead to the floor, and I wiped at my face with my kerchief, cleaning myself, forcing myself to reconstitute. My heart rate subsiding, I forced myself to my feet, groaning.

I went to the wall and ran my hands along it. Seamless, with no hint of the path that had been there only moments ago.

I returned, then, praying the entire walk that the passage remained. That I would find the stairway up again.

I found them, as evidenced by this transmission. Until I spied the long climb up, I had thought I would be a victim of Suffolk's trap.

I was right, about the snare, the great pitfall of the Architect's construction.

I was wrong, though, in my thoughts of its simplicity. It was not a simple creation. Or an easy one.

This will be difficult.

9

I saw it, Beloved. I saw your heart today.

I write today, but I truly do not know the day or date.

I delved again, under the bed. I thought it would be a brief trip. I had intended only to observe, to not truly explore. I had brought my notebook, and had packed a more robust amount of supplies, some short sundries and a large canteen, nearly a gallon of water. It was a heavy weight, and one I nearly left behind, in favor of my hip flask, which carries only a quarter of the liquid.

I thank you I brought the canteen, because without it I may not have returned alive.

I would call it a mistake, but because of it, I caught a fleeting glimpse of you, the truest part of you. And that is worth any amount of suffering.

I had intended to only range to a safe distance. I would make notes this time, of the doors, and the configurations of their constellations. Of the twists and turns of the halls near the stairs. If I could find a pattern in them, and if they truly ever turned on themselves. Were they random, or designed? And did the shifting gears and moving hallways happen often? What was the frequency of their movement, and was their design in it as well?

There were many questions, and I would need patience and study to answer any of them. I had embarked rapidly the day prior, and it had been a mistake.

I had exercised more caution, but I threw it away at the merest glance of you.

I counted the stairs on my descent. A thousand, precisely. Surely not a coincidence. But what does it mean? Anything at all? Another question for the Architect. But now I have a count.

The same door awaited me on my arrival to the maze, with the same pattern of four stars in the thirteen starfield. I made a crude marking in my notebook on one page.

I moved again to my right, but this time I marked my progress, tracing out a primitive map. Yes, it might move, but I would begin here. I must start somewhere, cannot allow the potential enormity of the project to dissuade me.

Not that it could, not anymore.

I did not venture far, not originally. I kept myself to the inner bounds, only a few minutes walk from the stairs, and if I hurried, I could retreat with haste. I would not risk being trapped, not after the scare from the day prior.

Even as I scouted, I was waiting. I checked my watch to see if the slowness of time was an isolated occurrence, taking notes on that as well.

But even as I paced through the close parts of the maze, I listened. Listened and waited for the great grinding shift, of the movement of the maze. How often did it shift? And were there some parts implacable, unmovable? Or was any part a potential clockwork, with no piece a sanctuary?

I also listened for the footfalls, but I did not hear any. Only my own.

I did not stay on the right path this time, also venturing to the left, and mapping out as far as a retreat felt possible. I encountered much the same as to the right, with the same wooden doors and walls. The layout was different, but not too dissimilar. I had yet to find any looping paths, however, or any dead ends. The maze continued in any direction it traveled, never doubling back on itself or stopping.

I encountered more doors and scribbled down their stars. All unique, with little overlap between which points were lighted and which were not. The constellations would require more study, I knew, not to mention I had yet to cross the threshold of any door. I truly could not know the constellations until I opened a door and crossed through.

But I could not broach one, not yet.

I mapped the halls as I could, but I was just waiting. Waiting for the gears to turn again, for the maze to shift once more, so I could comprehend its nature, perhaps predict it, perhaps even use it to my advantage.

Enough time passed again that a hunger overtook me, and I took the opportunity to eat, drink, and rest, sitting on the floor, my back leaned against the self-same walls, distant from a door or intersecting hallway. I ate until I was satisfied, leaving me with some rations remaining.

It marked the passage of time, my hunger, and perhaps was the only thing I could trust down there, my own nature, my own senses.

After eating, I thought to wander farther, to map farther out, but the risk of the day prior crept into my mind. I had set an arbitrary unit of time until I encountered another monumental shift, but what if it only occurred every few months, or was triggered by something beyond me?

Luckily, the issue was not pushed further, because the grinding of gears began, the floor shaking, and I tentatively moved closer to the stairs, away from the moving floors. I needed to know where was safe and where was not, and I saw the hallway rotate distant to the left, and as I hurried, another hallway closed off, distant and parallel to the hallway I walked in. Indeed, I saw the stairs now, and my proximity to them provided me with a sense of safety.

And then, just as quickly as the grinding began, it stopped. Had it gone faster that time? I made note to bring a stopwatch—but would it be hampered, as my watch is?—but soon all thought left my mind, as I wandered back toward the shift, to mark the difference in the maze in my notes.

I have already mentioned the feeling of your heart, of its proximity to me as I entered the House, as I moved within its confines. I felt it there, touching me, reaching out and placing your hand on my own vital organ, but a bolt of lightning struck me then, the same feeling of love and power amplified, multiplied, and it pulled my eyes toward its source, and a path had been cleared with this shift. A long hallway, a length I could not comprehend, farther than the one thousand stairs, a distance too far for the eye to see but my eye saw it an impossible feat but your heart provided the ability to me and I peered down the hallway of an inconceivable length and there was no thought only movement as I pushed my feet to their limit pumping my legs as hard as I could as a child runs toward its mother as a man seeks air when submerged.

I saw your heart, saw its resting place, on an altar, its final home, the place Suffolk had hidden it, had imprisoned it, and I would release you, hold you, finally. You waited for me, down that unthinkable distance, and I followed blindly, chasing as it pulled me, and I sweat as I breathed heavy, my heart pumping, and I pushed beyond my limits because you were there, you were there.

I ran for time untracked, and then the gears began again, but I had no caution, only you, even as the floors and walls shook, and disaster surrounded me, and then the maze shifted in front of me, and the lightning and thunder that lit my soul vanished in a trace, the impossible distance shortened, cut off entirely, a hallway ending and turning to the left.

I stopped in my tracks, covered in cold sweat, and looked back, and my retreat had been removed, the journey I had taken erased by the shifting maze.

I stopped, trying to catch my breath, to slow my breathing after the frenzied chase.

I couldn't panic, couldn't, and after a short moment, I breathed again, and I returned the way I came, taking a drink from my canteen, half gone now after hours in the maze.

I could puzzle it out, I could. I knew the direction of the stairs, I did, after staring at my notes, and if I ever turned toward them, I would find my way back to the stairs, and back to the surface.

I harried, hastening. The maze had shifted intentionally, baiting me with the greatest prize, setting the hook, and now I dangled, the barb firmly entrenched in my gums, and I would be reeled in now, dying in desperation deep inside the maze.

So I hurried away from you, as painful as it was, and turned toward the stairs, over and over again. If I turned toward them, I would find myself back at them, someway.

But as I paced, a road back to the ascent evaded me. Any time I turned back toward them, the hallway would turn again, farther away. I stopped, and retraced my steps, back to the long hallway, cut short, and I turned down a hallway going the other direction, hoping to find my way back.

But it got me no closer to the stairs, no matter how far I ranged, how much I delved, I found myself only farther—or at least what I thought was away.

My stomach ached, growling from hunger, and I stopped, sitting, and eating the last of my rations. It satiated me, and I drank. But only a little, enough to quench my parched throat, and then I reserved the rest. Another action that may have saved my life.

I sat in another hallway, all hallways, a door within view. I opened my notebook and scribbled its constellation, ten stars of thirteen, and their orientation. It looked like all the rest, all identical doors.

It was then I realized I could not explore the hallways, could not puzzle out this maze without delving through the doors. There would be no other way.

But I must regroup before then. I must escape this expedition, return upstairs, and come back better prepared.

I faced a binary. Should I return to the hallway that so tempted me, or should I continue to explore, looking for another path back to the stairs?

I only had water for supplies, a half gallon perhaps, and soon the energy provided by the rations I had just eaten would be gone. I must conserve energy. Delving any deeper would only doom me. It was a temptation, one the maze knew, perhaps even the Architect knew.

I returned to the long tunnel, to where it had been cut off from the stairs, and I sat at its terminus, and waited.

How much time passed? I do not know. I could not trust my watch, but I could trust my senses, and a terrible exhaustion washed over me. I should not sleep, I shouldn't have, could not rest when a shift could open up a narrow escape.

But my mind could not avoid collapse, and I slept fitfully, nodding off, and then I woke, woken by pangs of hunger. It ripped through my stomach. I had just eaten, had I not?

No, no, my watch said only three hours had passed, but it was a trick, the forces down here spoiling time itself, Suffolk using it against me. I drank only the water I needed, but it was soon gone, soon in the scheme of time, staring at the blank hallway, as I nodded off, as I waited, waited, prayed that the maze would shift back.

The great gears brought me out of a harried slumber, and I scrambled to my feet. The ground beneath me rumbled, and I moved off of the floor as it rotated, jumping to the unmoving segment of hallway just adjacent.

I watched it rotate, watched the hallway ending and turning to the right change in front of me, now facing straight again, the gears grinding around me, and the maze shook as it settled. I took a quick breath and moved down the hallway. It was the same, the same, and my heart rejoiced.

I found the stairs, the thousand stairs, and climbed them.

I encountered darkness when I emerged.

Safe. In Suffolk's House, but truly, it was all his. If I had learned anything from this expedition, is was that the maze was his as well, and if he was not piloting it from somewhere deep below, his spirit was, because it had used your heart as bait. To lure me, entrap me, and then kill me.

But he made a fatal mistake. Your heart has power over me, of course it does, but now that I've seen it, I will never stop.

Now that I know you are here, I will not quit until you are free.

10

Four days. I had been down the stairs for four days. If not for the canteen—I would not have emerged at all. I found the correct date when I went into town for supplies.

A canteen and a few rations will not be enough for a true expedition down the stairs. I must be prepared for days, weeks even, every time I embark down those thousand steps. I must let go of the notion that it will be simple or easy. The memory of your heart burned in my mind.

I did not want to leave the House, or step foot into Plainmoor, after the reception from my driver, or the folk at the train station, but the situation demanded it. It would have what I needed, and I couldn't waste more time traveling when your heart laid beneath my feet.

I had not truly seen the town, only the station and the surroundings as I was driven to the House. The same driver appeared, still beckoned by my good money, grimacing at the sight of the House, and eyeing me with bitter taste as I got into the vehicle.

As he drove, I saw the true state of Plainmoor. The driver had mentioned the illnesses and death, but the plague hadn't stayed isolated to the citizens, but had infected the town itself. The buildings we passed were decrepit and fallen to ruin. Paint flaked, glass broken, wooden siding crumbling. Boards covered over some windows, and old signs harkened to the businesses that once were, but now gone. I had thought the driver superstitious before, blaming the infection on Suffolk and the House. Surely, the Depression had caused this pain, not the presence of your heart.

The driver followed commands, and drove me into town, first to the grocery and dry goods, where most of my interests lied. I filled a cart with dried meats and fruits, nuts, and quick oats, along with canned fish and any other shelf stable items they carried, quickly amassing a few hundred pounds of variety. The scattered townsfolk in the store watched me as I shopped, not hiding their ire or idle curiosity.

Indeed, their hate-filled hearts reckoned me with utter disgust. I crossed past the newsstand in the grocery, hoping to grab a periodical or two for light reading, to distract me before bed, but a child sat there, reading a comic book. As I stepped up, the boy, no older than ten, considered me with dark eyes.

He only watched me, as he was missing most of his lower jaw. His chin was malformed, the skin pulled taut, and my eyes were struck by the unfortunate child. He stared at me, daring me to intrude on his reading, to ask what terrible incident left him like this, not that he could respond, but I did not need to ask. The driver had told me, had warned me.

Suffolk had brought it here, and it had spread to the town. This child was but another victim, and I left the newsstand, checking out with my food, and returning with my groceries to the driver, who helped load them into the trunk. He had parked on the curb, waiting for me to depart the grocer. A man with no arms sat on the adjacent bench, watching me. Bitter hatred poured from his eyes, but he said nothing.

"Are we to return, Mr. Collingsworth?" asked the driver after we finished loading.

"Does Plainmoor have an outdoorsmen store? Hunting, fishing, the like?" I asked.

"There's Wyman's," said the driver, not looking at me. "They are not as well stocked as they used to be—"

"It will do," I said. "Please, take me there."

The driver nodded and pulled away. It was only a short drive, where he again parked at the curb and waited for me.

The grocer had been one of the few buildings in town that had not yet fallen.

The same could not be said for Wyman's. The storefront was old, and the sign that graced the brick building had seen better days. Looking at it, it was not dirt or filth that stained the building, the sign, or storefront. It was entropy.

An older gentleman sat at the cash register and watched me as I entered. I did not feel hate or disgust emanate from him. Only weariness. I went to him.

"Could you help me, good sir? I need supplies for an expedition."

The gentleman spoke as if every word exhausted him. A tousle of silver hair stood on top of his head.

"I can help you, if we have. What do you need?"

I gave him my list, and he navigated his store, pulling down equipment and supplies from shelves and cupboards and stashes that no one knew but him. Rope and fishing line, hooks and bolts, bedrolls and thermal blankets. I did not know what else awaited me down those stairs, so I would prepare for any situation I could foresee.

The gentleman stacked my sundries on his counter, moving back and forth through his shop. After minutes of stacking, he stopped, moving back to the register.

"I have most of what you listed. No nets, sorry to say. Just no demand for them in Plainmoor. But aside from that, everything is here, accounted for."

"In good condition?"

"Yes, sir," said the man. "I know the look of the store, but I take pride in our stock. We don't sell faulty equipment."

I nodded, looking over the goods. They passed the eye test.

"I see you have rifles," I said, eyeing the back wall. "Do you have pistols? I would like the most powerful revolver you have."

He eyed me for a long moment, and then ducked down below the counter, pulling out something heavy, wrapped in soft cloth. He laid it on the counter.

"New on the market," he said. "Smith and Wesson Registered Magnum. Chambered for .357 Magnum cartridges. Can take down a bear, I've heard. Be careful firing it, it kicks like a mule."

"May I?" I asked, and he assented, a single nod toward me, and I picked up the weapon, and held it aloft. It was heavy, and I checked the cylinder, and then dry fired. It clicked hard.

"What do you think?" he asked. "I warn you. It's expensive. I shouldn't a bought it, truth be told, and the ammo is rich as well—"

"I'll take it," I said, and laid it on the counter. He rang me up, and I wrote him a check. The man moved quickly, with a sudden pep in his step. My spending may have made his year. He packed everything up, and helped carry it all to the car, filling the trunk and the backseat.

I don't like guns. I find them inelegant. However, I must be ready for whatever waits below me. My thoughts went to the distant footsteps that echoed back to me down there. If I encountered them, I'd be ready.

The driver took me back to the House. He still would not go inside, waiting in the car as I ushered my parcels through the front door. I did not push him. He was right to be wary.

11

The doors are necessary. I must become intimate with them.

It was clear Suffolk had manipulated magicks to construct the maze below. I could not confirm it, but its movements seem orchestrated. Either Suffolk or another was piloting its traps—or the maze itself was alive, watching, waiting, imbued with evil intelligence.

Either way, if my suspicions are true, the maze is an impossibility, unable to be constructed by man alone. The Architect, tapped into a magick, one unknown to me, and has utilized it to create his dire invention, his moving prison.

I do not recognize the hallmarks, am not aware of any that meld so well with the technology of man, but many exist, many beyond my keening, and any man who cannot see beyond his own nose and knowledge to recognize the possibility is a fool. And I am no fool. There are many magicks beyond me, and Suffolk used one, or several, the hypocrite.

For that's what he is. To think he dirtied his hands with what he once attempted to squelch. A miserable and pitiable man, who would so quickly employ what he once excoriated, once it suited his ends.

To imprison you, my love. I picture it in my mind, of Suffolk seeing the impossibility of containing you, of taking you, and finally realizing he must learn the skills he once despised, to accomplish such an improbable feat. The scoundrel, the scum.

The doors.

I have twice attempted to navigate the maze, and twice almost perished in my attempts. I could not avoid the doors, it was clear. They were a key piece of the puzzle. The doors, and the constellation engraved above them in brass.

Thirteen points. Above each door, the same engraving, brass, cast from some infernal furnace, with thirteen empty points, some dark, some lit. I compared my notes, my scribblings, to find a pattern of some sort among the engravings I had encountered so far.

And certainly, they shared certain points lit, and certain points dark, but finding a pattern was impossible, and furthermore, with the shifting nature of the maze, was a pattern even intended, as various doors would move, disappear, rotate. Indeed, my mind even thought to the fact of a second, or third maze, underneath the one I had traveled, an inverted labyrinth.

I pushed that thought aside. It would get me nowhere.

Looking at the constellations, I had some suspicions, some theories, but coming to any permanent conclusions was foolhardy. Indeed, it had nearly killed me days prior, when I so confidently strode back down below, thinking a gallon of water and two meals worth of rations would be sufficient.

An equal dose of caution and boldness would be required, because before I could come to any conclusion about the layout of the maze, the secret to finding your heart, and the hallways' connections to the doors, I would need to gather more information. I would need to see more doors, but more importantly, I must enter a door and see what waited for me inside.

So I packed the large rucksack I had acquired at the outdoorsmen mercantile. I carried gallons and gallons of water, along with two week's worth of rations that could be pushed to four if necessary. I loaded a bedroll, and rope, and various other small sundries I had obtained that may suddenly be needed.

I holstered the revolver on my belt, the heavy metal weighing on my right hip. But having it there made me feel safer. I did not know what laid on the other side of the door, and with the knowledge of the magicks Suffolk had traded in, I would be prepared for anything. The clerk had told me the Magnum could take down a bear if necessary. And mayhap it may be.

The rucksack was heavy, yes, but it would be lighter by the day, as I ate and drank, and I would rather carry the assurances on my back versus to my grave. And the pain I carried alongside—well, I would adapt.

I had decided, even before I disembarked, before I set foot down the thousand steps, which door I would open first.

There was no need to complicate matters, or to overthink it. I would open the first door, the door across from the stairs, the door that greeted me as I left the above and entered the below. I would start at the beginning.

I went down the thousand stairs, my ankles aching already from the added weight, but I pushed it aside, and soon found myself at the bottom landing. I had the brief concern of what if the door had vanished, removed by the machinations of the gearing maze, but no, it remained, perhaps always remained, the same constellation on display. It struck me that I could always trust the constellation. It would always tell the truth, the truth of the door. There was no cheating in that knowledge.

I paused, momentarily, listening, but there was only silence, the rhythm of my heartbeat, and my hand went to the knob, and I held it for one moment, and then turned and pushed through.

The door swung open, and a wave of salt air and sea foam struck me, the sound of waves crashing filling my ears. My vision was filled with a full vista of blue-gray, with white caps, the sea occupying my gaze.

I released the handle of the door, struck by what I saw. The ocean, the ocean, the sea, the sea. I had seen the Atlantic countless times, had been to many a beach, but nothing like this. As I swept my eyes from left to right, there was nothing but water, nothing but the white peaks of surging waves, of the steady pulling tide, as it washed in and out. All I heard was the water, the roaring crash of the water, the pushing constant feedback of water.

I stood on a beach, a stretch of sand that pushed beyond the edges of my vision to my left and to my right. The beach was forever, as was the water that met it. I looked out to the sea, looking for an island, a sandbar, a boat, any break in the infinite blue, but there was nothing, ocean as far as I saw, only water and sand.

I breathed deep, the salty air a welcome change from the musty odor of the House, of the fetid stench of Plainmoor. I could live here, on this beach, I could stay here forever, sleep on the sand, and fish for my meals, it would be a joyous life—

I blinked. This place, in just moments, had cast a pall on me, and I shook it away. It would keep me here forever.

I looked back, and the door I had entered through had vanished. I had taken only three steps, and released the door, and it was gone, and I was trapped, I would spend the rest of my days on this infinite beach, this meeting of earth and water, the culmination point, the beach would have its wish—

I settled myself, and took a deep breath of the salt and water. I could not condemn myself, not already, not after opening a single door. Was every door a trap? Was every door a portal?

I took another deep breath and took in my surroundings again. The ocean, and beach, both stretching beyond the limits of my eyes. I looked behind me and saw a dune that towered above me, fifteen feet high, covered in sawgrass and brush. There was no path up or through. No humans had walked this dune or broke a trail through it.

I would not broach the dunes, not yet. I stood midway between the dunes and the waves, the sand still cool and dry where I stood. Indeed, the beach was temperate, the sky a dark gray that mirrored the darkness of the water. It looked to threaten rain, but there was no thunder. The clouds did not move. Did the weather shift at all in this permanent place?

I walked down, closer to the water, the crashing of the waves getting louder and louder. As I approached, I better realized the scope of the sea, of the waves crashing onto the sand, higher than my head. To walk out into the water would be a death sentence. The strength of such water would overwhelm even the world's best swimmers. I toed the edge of the sand where the ocean met, but did not cross over, keeping my feet dry. I did not know what would happen when that threshold was crossed. I had tempted fate enough this day.

I looked again, to the left, and then to the right, looking for any landmarks, any sign of demarcation. I looked for wildlife, seabirds a hallmark of any beach I had ever visited, but there was nothing. There was no sound, nothing but the waves churning and crashing, breaking hard onto the earth.

Then I saw it, a twinkle to the right, a light at the edge of my vision, and I set off that way, toward it. Perhaps a trick, or a lure, but there was no way out that wasn't toward, and I set off, stepping on the sand. I walked, the ocean crashing to my left, salty wind buffeting me, but I continued. I looked for the twinkle again, my eyes up, but I did not see it.

As I walked, I finally saw something else. Someone else.

I saw the fisherman.

He stood in the dusky gray, distant at first, but with increasing clarity as I approached. He wore fishing gear, thick and warm to withstand the cold and wet, woolen with rubber boots. He wore no hat, long strands of thick white hair tumbling in the wind, but never in his eyes. His skin was a deep brown, dark and tanned, worn by the sun, the sun that did not exist here. He held a fishing rod, long, made with thick metal, with a massive reel, a size I had never seen, and the thick line extended out into the sea, disappearing into the high water.

I walked, watching him as I approached. He held the rod steady as the water tugged at the line. More rods stood in the sand, held aloft by tubes buried in the earth. More lines extended out into the water. A dozen lines, all thick, all tense, all disappearing into the dark.

I slowed as I got close. The man was armed only with his fishing rod, and did not seem a danger, but still, I did not want to surprise him. I do not know how he could not be aware of me, but I also did not see his vision leave the water.

So I stood near him, watching him fish. The wind howled past us, but it did not move him, as he quietly held his rod still, his eyes on his line, his hands holding his reel taut.

"Catch anything?" I asked, finally, the sound of my voice stark.

"No, not yet," he said. His voice was warm, a deep rumble that shook free from his chest and up through his mouth.

"I'm Henry."

"Charles, but you can call me Charlie," he said. "I apologize for not shaking hands, but I have a feeling about this cast."

"A feeling?" I asked. "What are you fishing for?"

"Oh, the big one," he said. "The One Which Dwells Beneath the Waves."

I said nothing, looking farther down the beach. Nothing lay past Charlie, nothing but more empty sand, and water that stretched out of sight.

"I—I'm, sorry to say, a little lost. Where exactly are we?"

Charlie nodded, softly. "You have that look about you. They come through, once in a while. I didn't intend to serve as guide, but they say a fisherman serves as many men."

"Well, if you do serve as a guide, could you tell me where I am? And if you know of James Suffolk and his House?"

Any sign of joviality left his face, a stark stare out at the water. "Aye, I know of Suffolk. The Architect. He's made a mess of it. And we're on the Beach."

"The beach. Which beach?"

"All of them," said Charlie, finally looking me in the eye. Silver glinted in them. Was it his eyes I saw, from so far away? Couldn't be. Must have been a hook or tackle, glinting in the sun. And wait—all of them?

"I don't understand."

"You won't," said Charlie, looking back at the water. "But that's okay. You're looking for a way out. Or in, I suppose."

"I mean, yes," I said. "The door I entered—it vanished, and I—well, I was left here, on this beach. Should I try and go up the dune—"

"Don't leave the beach," he said, his voice sharp. "Don't go in the water, and don't brave the dune. You will find more than you can reckon with."

"Well—then how do I—"

"Keep walking down the beach," said Charlie. "You'll find another door. A way out."

"Another door?"

"There's always two doors, young man," said Charlie. "Always two doors."

"How do you know that? Do you know about the maze? Do you know the key to finding—"

"I spoke to Suffolk, once upon a time," said Charlie. "Told me there are always two doors. Has to be. He didn't elaborate, and I didn't ask."

"What about the maze?"

"I don't know," said Charlie. "I don't leave the beach. Might miss the catch."

I said nothing. He had spoken to Suffolk, but Charlie was a man of few words.

"Did he tell you anything else?" I asked. "Please, it's of vital importance—"

"He told me he had big plans," said Charlie. "Like I said, he had just stopped through. Seemed a little nervous—but then again, so do you. Don't worry. As long as you stay on the beach, you're safe."

I had so many questions for Charlie, about this allbeach, about his fishing, about him, about his discussion with Suffolk. But Charlie only looked out at the sea. He spoke only in cryptics, and I must return to the maze.

But my goal is your heart, not the mysteries of a fisherman.

"A second door is down the beach?"

"Yes," said Charlie. "Always two."

I nodded. "Thank you for the information. Good luck."

"Thank you kindly," he said.

I walked behind him, toward this second door. I stopped. "If I come back through, will you still be here?"

"Hard to say," said Charlie.

"Then goodbye," I said, and I walked, and did not look back. I walked along the beach, the towering waves to my left, and the soaring dunes to my right. Don't leave the beach, Charlie had said. What lay beyond those dunes? More sand? Endless dunes, in direct proportion to the infinite ocean? Or something else?

My curiosity ached, but I resisted. Your heart is my mission, my quest. Other questions and riddles must not distract me.

I trudged along the allbeach, and after a time I spotted the other door, standing in the distance. I encountered no other creature or being on the way, and observed no birds. I heard nothing but the crashing toil of the water, and the howling salt of the wind.

The door stood freely, unsupported, and I did not stand on ceremony, seizing the door knob and opening it, swinging out, and then I was through, off the allbeach, and back in the familiar hallway of the maze below. I let go of the knob and the door shut soundlessly behind me, and I looked and there was only a door. I looked above, and the engraving matched my entry.

But the stairs were not in sight. I was somewhere else in the maze. Another door stood opposite this one. A different engraving.

I did not bother looking at my watch, for it would not truly tell me the time. But I was starving, ravenous, and desperately tired.

How long had I been on that beach? How long had I engaged in conversation with the fisherman? It had felt like brief moments, but my lips were parched, my tongue raspy.

I desperately drank and ate a measured portion of rations. I looked up and down the hall, the same but different from all the others. I would make camp here. I will sort out my thoughts tomorrow, and make my way further.

12

I have rested and regained my senses.

After leaving the beach, I slept, slept deeply, on the bedroll. It is only somewhat more comfortable than the hardwood floor, but I was so weary, so exhausted, that the roll felt as plush as a king's bed.

I stare at the door across. I stare at its constellation.

It sits across from the exit from the allbeach. It doesn't seem a coincidence.

The door to the beach, directly across from the stairs, and this one, across from the beach's exit. A direct line.

The constellation is five points, not four, all different points lit. I marked it in my notebook, alongside all the other constellations I have noted.

My theories of the engravings, and of which stars are lit and which are left dark, are more concrete after the allbeach, but I am still left with questions, questions that may be unanswerable, nested inside of each other.

The fisherman. The beach. Suffolk.

The fisherman said there are always two doors. Meaning an entrance and an exit. Always a way in, and a way out. There is always an escape, regardless of what I may find through any door. But clearly the doors are not bound by physics, not our physics, the magicks Suffolk utilized bound by other dark laws. I suspected as much before I opened the door, but I could not know without testing.

Questions have whirled through my mind since I left the beach. Questions about the fisherman. Who is he? He spoke of a great catch, of the one who dwells beneath the waves. Of the beach itself, of the dangers both in the water, and in the dune.

But I must push all those questions aside. For if each door truly broaches into another world, another time, or something undefinable, each will bring overwhelming questions, will draw me away from your heart and this maze. I must abandon them, truly, or I will be caught a thousand times, for your essence may be through a thousand doors, a thousand worlds, a thousand rooms I must endure before I see you again.

And I will endure them, if it is the only way.

So the fisherman, and the sea—I must let those mysteries lie, not until they stand in the way of you. But the fisherman knows nothing but the allbeach.

But no, that isn't true. He spoke of Suffolk. A meeting with him, once. When? Impossible to know, but I harken to guess a longer time than it seems, considering minutes on the beach almost famished me, exhausted me.

The fisherman said Suffolk had a plan. He also spoke of the mess the Architect had created. The maze itself? Perhaps. I should have questioned him more, but the sea's proximity had dulled my senses, something I did not realize until I escaped it. It had wanted me to stay. Perhaps fish alongside the angler, perhaps like many others, perpetually seeking a great catch, the One That Dwells Beneath the Waves—

See, I have already sought into a mystery I cannot answer. A dangerous place to be.

The door ahead of me. Is it truly a coincidence it is a straight line, ahead of the stairs? A direct path so far. Was it constructed by Suffolk, this alignment of doors? If my suspicions are correct, then no, it is impossible, no man could construct it, the permutations too great to calculate, the variations too large for any mind to hold at once—

But with the use of magicks—it was possible. Had Suffolk mastered one, or many? Or had the magicks used him?

I do not know. I feel Suffolk down here, and I do not think it is the residual energy of his construction. He remains in the House, in the maze. And I do not think I can escape this place, with your heart intact, without reckoning with him.

I still stare at the door across. The hallways go left and right, and upon small exploration, I see more doors, and their engravings and coordinates. I sketched them in my notebook. I could attempt them, and I may yet, but could the way through the maze be a straight line?

I do not know, but a deep anxiety has wormed its way into my stomach. I do not know what lies on the other side of this door. Is it another great sea?

Another maze?

Suffolk himself, waiting with a weapon to waylay me? To stop me on my grand and noble quest?

Perhaps.

But nothing ventured, nothing gained. I will keep my hand near my pistol.

I will speak to you again on the other side.

13

The enormity of the sea and infinite beach lingered in my mind as I stepped through the door, but I was confronted with something small.

My stomach ached after I finished my last missive, but I forced myself to pack my things together, to strap the pack to my back, and to walk to the opposite door.

I did not know what was behind the new door, and the unknown dug deep into my worry. But I forced myself, taking a hold of the doorknob and squeezing, my other hand on my pistol, and then I pushed through, swinging the door inward.

The room was small, only ten by ten feet, and I had told myself to not let go of the knob, to hold the door open until I had gotten a read on what I walked into, until I understood what I faced, but I let go regardless, and the door closed behind me.

A simple room, square, ten feet by ten feet. A carpet, also square, covered the center of the room. On that carpet sat a table, simple, wooden, also square. On that table were two objects.

A scale and a knife.

I waited where I stood, the door closed behind me. I looked past the table and saw the other door, directly adjacent. A straight line, still.

But the table, scale, and knife lay in my path.

I took a breath, and then another, but the scale did not move, nor did the knife, and I approached the table. The knife was simple, a chef's knife, one you would see in the kitchen, not on safari. The knife was clean and honed. As I drew near, light gleamed off the blade's edge.

I reached out slowly, my fingers trembling, and touched the handle, and then grabbed the knife, squeezing the wood in my fist. The blade's lightness surprised me, holding it. I stared at it, looking for anything strange, but it was simple, and sharp, and only a knife.

I put it down.

The scale stood next to it. It shone dully, inelegant, plated in brass. Unlike the knife, it was not normal at first glance. The right arm was down, touching the table, while the left was high, cocked. Nothing sat on its platform. Weighed down but empty.

My first instinct was to weigh down the left arm, to balance the scales.

But instead, I moved to the other door. Always two doors, and if it would let me move forward without playing whatever game was intended, then I would take the passage.

I grabbed the knob and turned, but the door was locked tight. I pushed and pulled, but it did not budge. I had suspected as much, but I had to try, and so I returned to the first door, and found the same.

My pistol was loaded with heavy rounds, and one shot would destroy any normal lock.

But I doubt any locks in the House are normal, certainly not down those thousand steps, and so I kept my pistol holstered.

I was to solve this puzzle, to balance this scale. Balance the scale, and the doors unlock? Seemed too simple to be true, but then again, the fastest path led directly through this scale.

I returned to it, and paused, taking a breath. How simple was it?

I put a finger down on the left arm and pushed. The scale did not budge. I pushed harder, and then harder still, but it did not change. Not so simple.

What was the knife intended for?

I took off my pack and opened my pouch. It held a compass, useless down here. The compass was hefty, the extra weight a boon when it was battered, able to withstand additional wear and tear. I placed the compass on the left arm's platform.

No movement.

I opened my pack, and pulled items from it, a variety of things I had brought on my expedition. Rations, my cup, my pocket knife, a length of rope, and on and on, putting the items on the table one by one.

Systematically, I tried them. No effect. The cup, the pocketknife, the canteen of water, the box of matches, a length of rope, a spare shirt—no movement.

Finally, the dried meat I had bought from the grocers. It was a small piece, leftover from my meal prior to entering. I placed it on the platform of the left arm, and it moved ever-so-slightly downward.

I put some of the other objects with it, but there was no movement. I returned them to the bag, and grabbed another piece of dried meat, a large sausage, enough meat to supplement multiple meals. I pulled it from my bag and placed it on the left arm. It dropped suddenly, all the way.

I removed it, taking the chef's knife, and cut it in half, continuing to test the amount of sausage, until the scale was balanced, with roughly two-thirds of the sausage on the scale. I went to the door and tried the knob. It turned freely.

I returned to the scale, and removed the meat, and tried the door again. Locked. I would have to leave my food behind. A high cost, but unavoidable. I put the sausage back, scooping up the pieces and bundling them up. I would need to be even more careful with my remaining meat rations.

I paused, eating one, enjoying the peppery bite of the dried meat. I had puzzled my way out. I moved on, and now I find myself on the other side, back in the hallways of the maze. I emerged from the door at the end of a long hallway, shaped like a cross, with halls leading to the left and right, and another straight ahead. And sure enough, there was another door all the way at the end of the straight hallway. Another straight shot.

My instinct was to continue on, to move on quickly to another door.

But several things halted me.

First, my promise to send on the other side. I have reached the other side, and so I speak.

Second, questions have sprung up in my mind from the room.

And finally, the smell.

As I have sent my accounts of the scale, a question arose in my mind, questions that were surfacing even as I puzzled out the logics of this scale.

Why sausage? Why did sausage satisfy the balance, but not water, or rope, or cloth, or metal?

And if this maze truly must be conquered to achieve your heart, how would any one person be expected to satisfy its demands? It was only by luck alone I had the meat it needed.

But I have realized even one with no meat rations at all could satisfy the scale. Could reset the balance.

For any delver would carry the ingredient necessary on their person, be it a finger, or toe, or chunk of flesh. The knife provided was razor sharp, and would do the work necessary. Otherwise, one would starve, trapped in that room, trapped with that scale and that knife.

But chance shined favorably today, and I had the meat necessary.

But even as I emerged from the exit door, I was bombarded with a horrible stench. The path afore me lay clear. I may still continue onwards, but I must first discover the source of the smell.

It smells like death.

14

I have located the smell.

    After resting for a few minutes and sending my last missive, I went out in search of the source of the stench. I embarked down the hallway to the middle of the cross, looking to the left and right. They did not end in doors, but had multiple intersecting hallways of their own.

    I took a deep breath, glancing down the central hallway, seeing the door, continuing the straight path, but the smell took precedence. It was an anomaly, especially in the maze proper. This wasn't confined to one room, which contained multitudes. And the memory of distant footsteps on my first expedition still echoed in my mind.

    I would return to this door.

    The deep breath was to center myself, but also to ascertain the direction of the smell. It came from the left, and I moved that way at a measured pace, my footsteps pounding on the wooden floors. I passed other doors and took note of their constellations, scribbling each down as I passed. With each, I was getting a better understanding of their variables. I would soon have fifty different sequences in my notebook, and I made a mental note I should examine them when I had reached the number.

    At each potential turn I passed, I smelled, trusting my nose. I had been born with robust senses, and down here, they were all I had. I did not turn, continuing on, making note of the directions I had gone. Indeed, I dug into the pouch on my belt and pulled a piece of chalk.

After my two early expeditions, where I nearly was lost forever, I would not lose my way again. I would mark my path with the chalk, and be able to find my way back, or at least recognize where I strayed, if I strayed.

So I marked the wall after the hallway, and continued following my nose, taking note of two more constellations as I passed, and then turned right down another hallway, but my nose was not required to know it was the correct path.

The blood led the way. Splashes of blood decorated the floor and walls, staining the wood. The smell was even stronger now, the smell of copper acrid in the air. And the smell of rot.

The blood had coagulated on the wood, and what once was a puddle had formed a matted clump. I stepped around it, avoiding it as I could, and I came to a T-junction, and to the left was more blood, and then I saw the corpse.

The blood I had seen already was minuscule compared to the carnage surrounding the body. The corpse had been mangled, nearly ripped apart, the torso pulled to pieces, the intestines and internal organs torn out and then open, spilling viscera and gore onto the hardwood.

I drew my handkerchief from my satchel and covered my face, the smell overpowering. The body had been in this state for days, maybe longer, and my eyes watered at the stench of death, and my stomach roiled. I swallowed down my disgust. I had read many a medical examiner's log in my studies, and this was no different.

This was no different.

I moved closer. I did not want to see the remnants of this man's body, but I needed to know.

His body was sprawled across the width of the hallway, but his face was turned away, and I reached out and turned it toward me.

It was Suffolk. The Architect.

I had never seen the man in person. I knew him from a single photograph before I had entered the House, but his pictures were scattered throughout the House above, and although looking older and more haggard, his face unshaved, I still recognized him. Whatever had killed him had left his visage unscathed, the smallest amount of blood splattered on his cheek from when his throat had been torn.

I looked around the body and saw no bag or pack. He had been carrying only what was on his person—unless it was taken from him after he'd been killed.

But whatever killed him hadn't been human. Even with my cursory knowledge, his death was the work of a wild beast, something savage, with teeth and claws. A tool of man did not tear or rend this flesh. This was the product of something wild.

Alarm rang in me, and I stood up, and looked past the body, and then behind me, listening intently.

But there was nothing. Suffolk had been dead for days, or even weeks, and whatever had killed him was long gone as well.

But the question of what had slain him still rattled me. What vicious beast would be down here?

The words of the fisherman rang back to me. Suffolk had made a mess of it.

In the construction of this place, had he awakened something? Had he let a creature loose? Had he caught notice of something beyond him, or me? I have read of such creatures and done my best to avoid their notice. If they were within reach down here, then I must be wary, before I end up like Suffolk himself.

His face was one of utter shock and horror. He had not expected his death. I reached out and closed his eyes.

And then I saw the device.

It was true, he carried nothing, but this was in him, embedded in his chest. Circular, metal, bearing the same thirteen marks that lay above every door.

It sat there, inert, attached to him. I reached out, grazing with my fingers. I held it in my hand, and it whirred, and fell from Suffolk's chest, leaving behind a bare wound, the lasting mark of its presence.

I grabbed it, holding it, and flipped it over, seeing the mass of whirring gears and anchor points. It was still for only a moment, and then vibrated in my hand, the inner workings of the device churning.

I nearly dropped it before placing it in my bag. I would consider it later. The smell of Suffolk was penetrating deep into me, and I couldn't stomach it much longer.

I had found myself pitying the man as I surveyed the wreckage of his corpse. I should not pity him. He had imprisoned you, captured you, and devised this hellish place as a cell. As an obstacle. I would not pity him. Now that I know he is dead, there is one less hurdle to clear before I locate you.

I left his body behind and returned to the exit of the scale. I would follow the straight path, and find where it led me.

15

I saw the great city, Beloved.

I did not tarry after finding Suffolk's body. I returned to the crossroads and continued onto the forward road. I noted the constellation above the door ahead. Seven points of light this time, sharing some of the previous two doors I'd entered. It also put my total count of engravings to fifty, and I made a note to study after I emerged.

If I emerged, I had thought, because truly, each door is a challenge, a danger, a threat. I could not let my guard down, no matter the results from preceding forays. I must be ready for anything.

But I truly could not be ready for what I encountered on the other side. I went through the door, firmly, with a threaded determination, and the door closed behind me, softly latching.

I found myself in a hallway, but one unlike the one I had just left. The floors were magnificent tile, a golden etching between the stark white, with more thin veins of gold running through the white stone. Elegant white columns of the same stone stood, with more gold etchings, three pair, six columns, across from each other.

On my left was stone wall, great slabs of the same white and golden stone. Ensconced on each was a glowing torch, lit by some otherworldly source. They too glowed golden, the light sparking the veins of ethereal yellow that lined all the bone white stone.

On the right were three openings into the open air, and I saw only darkness from my perspective. I would have to move forward to see more.

Directly ahead of me, the matching wooden door stood stark in the bone white wall. A short passage through this world, entrance and exit again across. But I paused. Was it this simple? The scale had seemed simple, and indeed it was simple, at its core, but it was not easy, and I hesitated.

Before I moved, I tested the door behind me. The knob turned. I was not locked here, not imprisoned, at least not at first glance.

I crept forward, taking slow steps, letting my senses guide me. The smell was old, the scent of a library or bookstore, with books on the verge of dust, taken by the smell of paper on the brink of rot. It was sickly sweet, of a dark rum, of burnt sugar, of a candy left too long on the flame.

I walked through the first set of columns and I peered to my right, through the opening, into the open air, and I caught my first sight of The Yellow City.

I could not breathe.

The towers soared above me, twisting into domes, spires topped with the Yellow Sign. Walkways intersected below me, spinning off in webs in every direction, connecting buildings, all white, all gold, shining brightly in the dark. The gold glowed, blinding me, but I could not look away, and my eyes scanned the stretching city, boundless in all directions. The spires stood like pockmarks, each with the Sign, each serving a beacon.

I moved to my left, to the central opening, so that I saw more, but I still saw no boundary, no end to the city, only more spires, more walkways, more white stone buildings, each ornate and glowing, each a monument.

I had read in my studies, of this place, of this great city, but I would never imagine seeing it with my own two eyes. The scholars had only caught glimpses, after digest and study, after manifestation and ritual. But here I stood within, oh a wondrous sight!

I looked out, over the Yellow City, and I saw further, further, the endless metropolis, the great city, the otherworldly nation-state, and inside, the city crept into my mind, as I saw more and more, I saw the full extent of this place, the extent of his rule, as my eyes crept further and further within its boundless borders, the spires above me, above the dark clouds, the Yellow Sign penetrating into the space beyond, and I saw the rot and ruin and the desolate population, boiled away to sugar and dust, the sweet remains taken by the Kingin Yellow and I knew I must go now, or I would stay forever.

The city lay in front of me, the spires soaring, and I turned away. If I looked again, there would be no quest, no rescue.

Your heart pulled me away.

Had Suffolk seen this? Had he ventured here? Is this how he stole your heart? Had be magicked himself to your hiding place, and found you there, and stole you through a door? Had he built this first, and then committed his heist?

I do not know, but I tore my eyes from the cityscape and forced my halting legs forward, looking toward the exit door, and only it. The City drew me back, but your heart pulled me away, and your heart was victorious, as it ever is, as it ever is.

I opened the door and stepped through, and realized my heart thumped against my chest, my blood boiled, and my breath came halting. The City had almost taken me, had pushed my body into overdrive, and only your heart had saved me.

The Yellow City, a great place, of power and desolation in equal measure. But the Sign nearly had taken me, as it has taken so many others.

I must rest.

16

I have collected myself and have taken stock of my surroundings.

The door to the Yellow City stays firmly shut behind me. I exited into a hallway, of course a hallway, but one of a unique construct, a particular arrangement of wood and doors. For across from this door are three more doors. I had yet to see any doors arranged so close together, only a bare width of feet between each door. And the hallway spanned to my left and right a long distance, each ending in a T-junction, turning to the left and right themselves.

After I felt myself again, I sat and drank some water, and ate a small ration of dried fruit, and then took out my notebook, writing down the constellations of the three doors. Each different, with only a few overlapping similarities of their stars.

Three stars.
Nine stars.
Five stars.
Further evidence for my theories.

As I saw door after door in my expeditions, I have dutifully written their constellations. Which of the thirteen voids are lit, and which are dark. Co-ordinates of a sort, presumably, an identifier, a label.

I have seen no duplicates, not in over fifty sighted, except for each engraving's matching pair on their exit. I expect to find no two the same, no matter how long I stay here in this accursed maze.

I pore over my notebook, looking over the constellations, the different arrangements. I sort them, arrange them, count them in different orientations, categorize them by how many stars they have, or where they are located among the thirteen voids, but among each they only share a handful of similarities. Finding a trend, or any sort of through line seems impossible, not unless I investigate and catalog every door, which seems a fool's errand.

But of the thirteen voids, each can be lit or unlit, darkened or bright, each a binary, without regard if any other combination has been lit on another door. So, each void may be lit, or may not be, each unique combination a new address.

Math was never my strong suit, but I think I remember enough from the education in it I've received, and I believe it to be a factorial. A factorial of thirteen. After checking my math, the number is six billion, two hundred and twenty-seven million, twenty thousand, eight hundred. 6,227,020,800. Over six billion rooms.

The number is not infinite, but it is functionally so. No man could explore that many rooms in a lifetime, if indeed there is that amount down here. It is a number I cannot verify. Truly, the only man who could is Suffolk, provided he is responsible for this maze, and these rooms.

The number casts everything into question. How could Suffolk create such a place, even with the use of magicks? How could he tether that number of places to a single hub? Did he blindly reach out and lasso the many realms into this maze, linking them with doors of his creation?

I do not know. It is beyond me, and seems beyond any mortal man. And surely, Suffolk was mortal.

And surely—wait—

I was interrupted. Even now, my heart is still pounding. As I sent, I heard footsteps, distant, echoing from the right. And if there truly are that many doors, any other living being is a source of potential knowledge—or danger.

So I sprung to my feet and ran after the sound, leaving my pack behind. I kept my right hand near my pistol, and as I reached the end of the right hallway, I followed the sound of footsteps to the left. I reached out with a piece of chalk and marked the wall as I turned. The footsteps then moved faster, instead of walking, now running, but they were louder now, and I sprinted after the sound.

I marked as I turned down each hallway, moving too quickly to remember the turns, and I caught a glimpse of a shadow move down a hallway hurriedly, and I ran harder still, my lungs struggling to keep up, my heart thundering in my chest.

The footsteps I chased were not even, a broken rhythm, and I saw the figure lope ahead of me.

"Wait!" I shouted, but the figure did not stop, turning a corner. I turned after it.

"Curse you, wait!" I yelled again, and it stopped as it turned, and I saw the figure clearly.

It was a man, or once was. His face was distended, his jaw swollen, his hands wrapped in bandages. His torso was bloated, deformed, strange protruding growths swelling his ragged clothing. He stared at me with wild eyes, and then ran down the hallway.

"Please, stop, please," I yelled, but it came out in a hoarse gasp, my breath all but gone, and I ran again, my legs pumping with what energy I had left. I turned and saw him, but now he was waiting for me, his mutated face staring at me with venom and violence, and his hand moved to his hip, and on instinct I drew and fired my pistol, the gunshot booming in the halls, and then the ground was shaking, the floors shifting, and I would be caught adrift, and I turned, and ran, and the figure went the other way, my shot must have missed him.

I sprinted back to my rucksack and my supplies, and the walls shifted behind me, the floor tilting, and I ran and dove and the hallway was gone, as was the figure.

And so I sit here, again, the sweat still drying on my skin. Another lone, lost figure, mutated and nearly unrecognizable as human, who would not stop for me. Who ran at the sight of me. Was it a man at all, or only something that once was a man? Was he the one whose footsteps echoed in the maze?

I do not know, but he is gone, lost to me. I will not stay here long enough to see him again, if the shifting maze ever returns to that orientation.

I am still confronted by three doors, in sequence, across from the exit from the Yellow City.

The device that had been in the corpse of Suffolk is shaking, vibrating in my pack.

My first instinct is to follow the straight path and use the door directly across from the exit. But the fact there are three doors, so close together, somehow implies to me a choice is necessary. The lady or the tiger, which would it be?

And what did the device's vibration mean?

I have turned it over, and studied it. When I found it on the chest of Suffolk, it was not shaking, was not moving at all. Not until I touched it did it come alive. It bears the thirteen stars, the same constellation, but none are voided space. None of them will be light or dark.

And now, as it shakes in my hand, the underneath has opened, and inside, whirring gears move, even at incredible speed. I do not know what powers it, but I see now how it had attached itself to Suffolk. I saw the clamps and machinery, that would attach to skin, and tighten until it was unmovable.

But why would Suffolk have such a thing? Had he designed it? Had he built it? It bore the mark of the constellation, of the doors.

The thought struck me then.

Suffolk could not navigate the six billion doors of the maze, if he did indeed create this place, just as any mortal man would be unable. He would need a guide.

He would need a compass.

And my first thought would be to the unnecessary steps of creating something that attached to a body, that bled you.

But perhaps that was the only way.

The compass whirs next to me as I commune with you. It does not seek my skin, a home on my body. It requires me to attach it. To place it, to make the choice.

Can it guide me to you, at the mere cost of attachment? To pay blood and pain, and I have my compass?

I do not know. Nothing here is what it seems.

I have replaced it in my bag. I will make this choice on my own. The compass must wait, wait until I have pondered it further. And decided what costs I will pay, and if the return is true.

I have decided on the forward door. I will send to you on the other side.

17

Death. There was only death behind the door.

The Yellow City, for its decay and rot, was clean and glowed golden, the scent of burnt sugar clinging to my nostrils as it lured me into its infinite, unspooling wiles.

When I opened this door, I found myself in a world of flesh. The door fell out of my grasp, gone. Vanished.

But that is incorrect. It had not vanished. It had transformed.

It took me a moment to understand, my eyes still adjusting to the red. Because the space glowed with an unearthly red, no lights visible, no lantern, no electric light, but everything a crimson that filled my vision.

But then I realized the membranous pulsating sphincter was the door I had entered. It glistened in the crimson light, covered in some sort of thick liquid, and I hesitated to touch it, not even sure how to open it.

I turned to survey my surroundings and saw I was inside of some tremendous organ. The walls were flesh, various shades of pink and red, fibrous and muscled, with thick wide overarching beams of bone or cartilage. The floor itself was a springy, tongue-like material that moved as I stepped on it, my weight impacting it like a mattress. The space was enormous, a massive cavern, a cave of flesh I couldn't see the end of.

Staring out into the red glow of the cave, I realized further ahead of me lay something different, not a piece of the flesh I stood on, but a darker substance, a deep red.

The smell was not one of blood, not of copper and metal, but of putrid rot, of the deathly stink of gangrene, of flesh sloughing off the bone of the nearly dead.

And then I saw I was not alone in this cavern of flesh.

Bodies, bodies stacked and piled above my height. Moldering, rotting, decaying corpses, piled on top of each other, some nearly skeletons, others freshly dead, but all corpses, all dead. Everywhere I looked I saw them now, the red glow of this organ I found myself in showing me them.

They were not human corpses.

They were humanoid, of a sort, but their bones were thicker, larger, their bodies stooped, their faces craven, like a rat. My curiosity picked at me to get closer to one, to examine it, to see the difference, for the study, for the science, but my stomach pulled me back, kept me from them.

I should not touch them, could not touch them. I needed to find my way out, needed to be clear of this place. This was a place meant not for me, and my existence screamed in revulsion.

Move forward, my mind shouted, and so I forced my feet onward. I wanted to retreat, to push through the fleshy passage behind me, but I needed to move if I was to ever find you. You might be on the other side of this.

I had engaged on a journey of a straight line, and so on a straight line I would continue. I moved, the flesh pulsating under my feet, and I walked across this landscape of meat. The cavern was enormous, but I saw it was not infinite, the bounds of the walls covered by stacks of the dead others. But as I moved, I saw why the ground ahead of me was a dark crimson, the darkest shade present in this maroon grotto.

It was not solid flesh at all, but liquid, the dark blood of whatever this place was.

I stood on the shore of a bloody lake, and I looked across, and I saw the distant coast. I saw the pink tongue-flesh on the other side of this body.

And I saw the door.

Traverse the lake of blood, and I could move on.

But there was nothing to carry me across. There was no boat, no raft, no ladder, no bridge.

I eyed the nearest pile of bodies, and slipped on the pair of gloves I had, and one by one, dragged them to the shore. Pieces of flesh came off in my hands, and I flung them away, swallowing back my disgust, the bile rising in my throat. I must not vomit. My rations were too valuable to waste.

I dragged corpse after corpse over, not studying the difference in their physiology, keeping my eyes from focusing on them. I pulled a dozen corpses over, my lungs straining, breathing in this biologic air, and I pulled the rope from the bag, and strung them together. I had made a wager in my mind to this process, and I hoped it would pay dividends. Otherwise, it was for nothing.

My knots were tight, and the bodies were bound. And then there was only to see the soundness of my wager, and I pushed the bodies out onto the crimson liquid.

They floated, and I breathed again, and I scrambled aboard, my boots splashing through the shallows. I floated on a raft of the dead, and I pulled out my small unfolding camp shovel, and I paddled with it, sliding it through the lake of blood. It was slow progress, but it was progress as I paddled.

I kept my eyes forward, no different from a canoe journey I would make as a child, paddling with my father on the pond near my childhood home. No different, I told myself. I did not look at the piles of corpses, or the viscera that floated in the liquid beneath me.

I kept my eyes forward, drawing ever closer to the exit. The exit, free of this accursed place, this hell of meat.

But then a great noise from above me sounded. The sound of a massive sluice, of pipework, of plumbing.

But there was no metal here. Only a terrible throat, and I looked above to the sound, and saw another orifice open, and thousands of corpses fell from it, in a gout of flesh and blood.

I only had a moment and I paddled desperately away, but they spilled onto my raft, knocking me off, pushing me down underneath the surface, and I took a desperate breath and closed my eyes, holding tight to my shovel, and my tenuous grip on it was the only thing that saved me.

The bodies forced me down, and I swam, my pack heavy, but buoyant, and it saved me as well, and I swam to the side, hoping to find the edge of this monstrous intake of new meat, and I felt their hands and arms and legs and feet and faces, their torso, their skin, their organs, submerged in this lake of blood, and I fought through it all, you, you were what saved me. Because I imagined you, somewhere deep inside this hell, and I would rescue you, I would save you, and this abattoir would not be the end of me.

I swam, I swam, I desperately swam, my lungs aching, my breath at an end, but then the swarm of bodies from above was not on me anymore, and I paddled to the surface of the horrible lake, and I reached it, and I pulled in a desperate breath, my lungs screaming in pain.

But I could not stop, the torrent of bodies and blood from above continuing, expanding, and I realized the base of this great lake was bodies, a mountain of bodies below a lake of blood and I swam hard, stroke after stroke, the far pink distant shore, and I did not stop to let my disgust register. I only thought of your heart.

My own pounded as I swam, pushing myself to my limit, but I needed out, I needed escape, I needed exit, and then I was there, on the tongue-shore, and I stepped out, my body and clothes soaked with gore and blood.

I thought to look back, to consider this hell and what it was, but I pushed toward the membranous flesh-door and pulled at its opening, and it cascaded open, and I went through.

18

The smell still clings to my nostrils.

I have since cleaned myself as well as I can. I wet a rag with the water I could spare, stripping down to the nude, and wiping as much gore, blood, and viscera off me as possible. I changed into my one pair of fresh clothes, throwing my soaked clothing to the side. It is ruined, and nothing will change that. I could dry it, and wear it, but the smell would cling, and I would lose my mind with that clear stench following me minute by minute.

I thought briefly to the fisherman's ocean of dark water, where one does not stray, but I'd gladly chance the danger, and trade the saltwater for the blood that was quickly drying on my skin.

I examined my rucksack, as it had been soaked in the terrible sea, but luckily it had been fastened tight, waterproof, and the exterior was resistant to the liquid as well. But my bag was lighter still, the rope gone, the change of clothes worn, a quarter of my rations eaten, a quarter of my water drank, or used to clean my skin.

I had emerged from the cavern of flesh, the meat pit of bodies, back into another hallway. Another damnable hallway, same as it ever was.

But this time I faced an array of nine doors, all across, all aligned, all facing the singular exit.

A singular exit. The other two doors. The left and right. Where did they exit?

Not here. No matter. I made it through the test of flesh. For this, all was a test. A puzzle. A game. Because what else could you call the nine doors in front of me? I must decide which path to take, which room to enter, which world to delve. The right path would take me closer to you, while the wrong would lead me astray.

Or worse, kill me. Or even worse, condemn me to something beyond my imagination, a pain and punishment worse than death.

But I did not pause to reconsider, or to send you a devotion. I made a choice, the same as I have before, the direct route, the straight path. I would follow it to its conclusion, and move quickly, before my nerves would force me back. To return up the stairs, out of this fresh hell.

I opened the door, and it shut behind me. I hoped to hasten through the room, hoped it would not be another room of otherworldly horror.

I was not confronted by the smell of death, a cavern of flesh, bulbous muscle surrounding me, in the great blasphemous stomach of some terrible thing.

No, I did not know what I saw.

It was a room, I thought, at first, a simple room, not too different from the scale and knife, simple wooden construction, a door across, but as I blinked and moved and breathed, my eyes could not take in what I saw.

I looked across this room, for the exit, for the way out, but I could not find a door. I could not find a straight path forward, I could not find forward at all.

Angles. I saw right angles, turning, turning; the walls bending to the right, forward, turning to the right, and then where a door should be was another right angle, but it made no sense, it turned toward me, but then another right angle, always right angles—

This is where I realized, and I closed my eyes, shut them tight.

It saved my life.

I sensed them there, immediately springing from the meeting of things, where corner met corner. I don't know how, because they did not breathe, not in the human sense. But I felt them just as the air settled around one in a graveyard, where the darkness lie in a misbegotten library.

You can feel the wrongness, the alien nature of the thing, and I felt the Hounds there, surely as your heart reached out for me, somewhere deep inside the maze.

The Hounds. I sensed them there, prowling those infinite right angles, into this trap I had stumbled into. I had been lulled, thinking the straight path was the correct one, and the Hounds had sprung from outside of place, moving in, but I closed my eyes, had not spotted them.

I breathed shallowly, I knew they prowled the room, stalking anyone who would spot them traversing through time and space, through the bending of dimensions, but if I did not see them it would not be a trespass, would not be the end of me.

For I now knew what had killed Suffolk. He had seen the Hounds, in one of the jaunts he had taken on his way to and fro, between the multitude of rooms in your imprisonment. Maybe it had been a single time, early in his journey, or it had been a simple misstep late, his eyes open when they should not have been.

Either way, he had spotted them, and he had fled, running from the room, closing the door, hoping it would be enough.

But there was nowhere to run from the Hounds, no matter how many steps you took, how much distance you traveled. They would follow, follow tirelessly, run you down and rip you to pieces, and then vanish back into the lines and angles.

I felt them there, and I reached back behind me, my eyes still closed, and I blundered through space, hoping I wouldn't touch one, hoping desperately, because touch was another form of discovery, another way to see, and my hand groped desperately until it touched wood, and then the metal knob, and I prayed it was not locked, and it wasn't, and I emerged back into the hallway, with nine doors, facing me.

I did not open my eyes again until I heard the door firmly shut.

19

I have sat here waiting in the hallway. I waited, I listened.

I did not see the Hounds, the accursed beasts. I did not perceive them. I only saw the signs, saw the hints of their environs.

But I did not perceive them. For that is a death sentence. They killed Suffolk, surely. Ripped and torn, his stomach and throat, his intestines spilling out onto the wooden floor. He saw them down here, and they found him.

Did Suffolk know they were hunting him? Had he studied enough? Had he read?

I don't know. But I didn't see them, so they did not see me, the rounded pupil of the eye antithetical to their existence, an affront to their being.

But that is hearsay. The only words written about them are by men who have been hunted and killed. And how do you trust the research of someone underneath a dangling sword?

But I cannot go back through that door. If there is an exit, somewhere inside the infinite right angles, I would never find it, and I surely could not do it without risking the ire of the Hounds.

If there is an exit, I was meant to witness the Hounds, and doom myself to the endless hunt, regardless if I escaped.

I have been waiting for a trap to spring, my eyes up, searching for evidence, but it is clear now this is all a trap, not just for your heart, but for anyone inside. Each room is a potential death, each hallway a possible end. I was a fool to think a forward path would be enough to find my way to you.

I feel you there, I do, reaching out to me. But I can't follow it, no matter how I try.

I don't want to use the compass. I don't want to use something Suffolk created, a crutch, more than he constructed, a device that was a part of him, attached to him, another organ or limb.

I hesitate to think what it would do to me. Is it just another trap, another snare, another trick? It shakes and vibrates still, and I stare at it, its whirring and snatching gears inside, ready to work.

But I do not know what else to do. There are eight other doors here, and two hallways that turn upward from me, the left hallway to the right, and the right hallway to the left, and looking down either I see more hallways, spinning off to the right, and within an hour they will shift again, stranding me in some unknown place.

I stare at the device, if indeed that is what it is. I believe it to be. I need guidance. I need a path to you.

I will be attaching the compass.

20

I have a compass.

It came at a cost.

The device whirred in my hand, larger than my palm. It was attached to Suffolk's chest, and I would place it similarly. I unbuttoned my shirt, and pulled it open, and lowered the vibrating device to my breast, above my right nipple, near my shoulder.

I haltingly lowered it, breathing slowly, but when it touched my skin, it went into action. The gears inside it, the moving metal, it shot out, and latched onto me, and the pain ripped through, and I bit down hard on the belt placed between my teeth.

But it did not stop with a simple clamp, the gears than pulling skin and muscle inside it, ripping, tearing at my skin, and blood poured down my torso, and I hastily wiped at it with a rag, even as the shock overwhelmed me.

I could not lose consciousness, not in this place. I could not be without control of myself, no matter the length of time. It squeezed, and then punched itself into me, becoming a part of me, and I lost all my air, and then I passed out, the torment too much to bear.

I woke up momentarily with blood in my gums. I had bitten my tongue in my distress, and it stung. The pain in my mouth was small compared to the deep ache in my chest. I pulled out the pocket mirror from my side pouch and looked at it from ahead.

The device had embedded itself in me, another organ. I tentatively touched it, the cold metal already warming from its close contact with me. Indeed, blood was flowing through it, my blood feeding it, or powering it, the magicks working with my life essence.

Horror overtook me for a moment, Suffolk's creation buried inside me, my blood flowing through it, now a part of me, inextricable, but then I felt it.

As it warmed, as my blood flowed through it, it tugged on me. A gentle pull, a magnetism. A guiding hand that showed me the precise route.

The path to you.

I stood and walked down the hallway. It was simple now, a clear marker for the correct path. The compass pulled me toward the door to the left of the straight road.

But then again to the door on the right.

I tested again. The feeling was the same. Did both lead to you? Was there something else I was missing?

There was no feeling for any of the other doors, including the door I had already entered, that contained one of the many homes of the Hounds.

I packed my things together again, and picked the right door, for I am right-handed.

I opened it with confidence, but still with trepidation. Just because it was the correct path did not mean it was easy.

What test would await me? What must I feed the room before I can pass through the other side? Must I swim through a lake of blood again?

No, this room was quite mundane in its construction. It was a simple room, this time, perhaps twenty by twenty feet, with flowery wallpaper covering the walls, an oriental rug on the floor. An ornate light hung in the center of the room, but it was otherwise undecorated.

It was not the only thing inside, however, because again I found myself accompanied by death.

Dead bodies were stacked to one side of the room. There was a faint odor, but it was relatively mild, compared to the ungodly stench of the cavern. It was an old smell, antique, the scent of a body long since rotted.

Indeed, these corpses were long dead. Some were nearly skeletal, all dead for months or years, the skin and flesh dessicated, abandoned by rot. And they were not numerous beyond count. There were six of them, stacked three high, rather neatly.

They still wore clothes, although the clothing had rotted as well, the fibers wasting and tearing.

I moved closer, studying them. They were all human, all men. All piled neatly. Cause of death was impossible to ascertain, as the bodies were far too old, but all had all their limbs. There was no catastrophic damage to them. And even then, with the age of the bodies—cause of death would be indeterminate at best.

I looked around the room, looking for anything else of note. Nothing, except for the decorations previously mentioned, and the two doors, the entrance and exit. Looking again at the bodies, none of them carried anything but their clothes on their backs. Searching through their pockets, I found nothing. No ID, nothing identifying.

Why were they here? Who were they? There was no sign of struggle in the room, or any amount of violence to it. They were dead before they were brought here. Killed in the maze?

But that's impossible. How would six others know of this place? I would have learned of them, I know it, somewhere along the way.

I do not understand all the magicks of the hallways, but I have recognized these doors are portals, portals to otherworldly places, that have no context to their placement in the maze. This surely must be that, even if it is an odd one.

Six bodies. Stacked neatly.

I looked at them again, hoping to see something I missed, but there was nothing. I thought to retreat, and go through the door on the left, and see what it held. But it was only a thought. Because each door contained any amount of menace, and I must not push my luck. With the compass, I have a gift horse.

I vacated the room and found myself back in the maze, in a hallway. But no line up of doors. Only a varied hallway, leading off in two directions, which leads to many more.

There is a feeling of progress. With the compass, I am no longer lost.

I must rest. I will speak again.

21

I speak to you having met the Lover.

He interrupted my rest, strolling around a corner of the adjacent hallway. I waited, my pistol ready, waiting for whatever emerged.

The Hounds, of course, dominated my mind. I hadn't seen them, but maybe I had, maybe my eyes had caught a glimpse, and they had tracked me down.

They would kill me, but I would not go quietly. Would my bullets damage them? A question I could not answer, but I would try, try to stop them with whatever defense I had.

I had thought Suffolk was the footsteps I had heard early in my expedition. He was dead. There was also the other misshapen man I had seen, had fired at. Had he come back, back to see who I was, who had attacked him?

The footsteps echoed to me, closer and closer, and I waited patiently, the pistol heavy in my hand, my arm aching, and then the man turned the corner. I thought it Suffolk for a moment, but that was impossible, and then he came into view and it was clear it wasn't Suffolk, nor the man-monster I shot at in the shifting maze.

He was not surprised to see me. He smiled wide, his grin baring teeth. His hair was long and haggard, a dull silver, and it swayed in front of his face. He pushed it back and away to look at me. He wore no shirt, or shoes, his pants brown cloth, with a simple belt. His feet were filthy, covered in muck. A knife was sheathed on his side, but he carried nothing else. How did he survive down here?

"Well, hello," he said, approaching. My pistol was still aimed at him, but he approached, undisturbed. "A new pup, I see. Fresh into the grinder, eh?" His voice was deep, every word a growl.

I said nothing. What could I say?

"You can lower your shooter, son," he said. "I won't hurt you. Always nice to see another devotee."

I lowered my gun, but I did not holster it. This wild man had caught me unprepared.

"Cat got your tongue, pup? What's your name?" He had stopped, settled, six feet away, but there was a nervous energy in him. His feet subtly moved even as he stood still.

I took a breath. "Henry Collingsworth. I own The House. Who are you?"

He laughed, a loud, brash laugh, his rib cage shaking. I would say he was lean, but that only painted half the picture. An accurate description was that he looked hungry.

"You own it, eh? What happened to Suffolk?"

"I found his body. Torn apart," I said. "You spoke to him?"

"Of course," he said, still smiling. He wouldn't stop smiling. It would drive me mad. "Torn apart, you say? Thought he was smarter than the Hounds. Foolish of him. Although—maybe I'll see him around. I'll try to warn him." He stared away, his smile finally dropping, but then it returned, lost briefly in a valley of the mind.

"Warn him? It's far too late for that."

"Yes, of course," he said, smiling even wider, but then it shrunk, the ebb and flow of his lips and teeth flowing quickly.

"Your name?" I asked. The man was maddening.

"Oh, yes. A name. Elias. Elias Morgan. Forgive me for not shaking hands." I saw his fingertips were stained black. More filth, at a glance, but I studied for a moment longer and it was not muck that blackened them. Something else. "I've dipped them in the salt sea, one too many times. Better not to spread the Dweller."

The smell of him wafted over to me by then, his scent strong. He smelled of musk and filth, a deep stink of body and sweat and dirt. He clearly had not bathed in many a day.

"How long have you been down here?"

"You'll learn," he said, his grin not wavering.

"What?" I asked. He stood six feet away, but he towered over me, on top of me.

"You'll learn that question is inadequate, pup," he said. "Long enough. I've yet to find her. I've gotten close, and I'm getting closer still. You think that will help?" He nodded toward the compass.

Find her? You? How? Was he on the same quest? There is no way, I was the only one.

"It has already saved my life," I said, not knowing how to answer. "I needed a guide."

"You took it from Suffolk," said Elias. "Did it serve him?"

"I—"

"No compass will stop the Hounds, this is true," he said, interrupting me. I was tiring of this man. My hand still held my pistol. He tapped his chest. "My heart will lead me to her. It is only a matter of time."

I said nothing, my heart seething. He spoke of you in such a familiar way.

"I have spoken to her, you know. She led me here," he said. His smell was in my nostrils, and hot anger rose in my chest. How dare he speak such blasphemy. You? Speak to him? Impossible. "I love her. I will complete her. I will rescue her."

My nose rankled, my grip firm on the pistol. I could raise it, fire, and shoot him dead. He looked away from me, bemused, thinking of you, clearly. How dare he, this Lover!

"You do not know her," I said, finally. He glanced back at me, his eyes blazing. His smile remained, shrinking, then growing enormously.

"I wish you well, pup," he said. "But I must go to her." And then he moved, his nervous feet walking past me, without a second glance, and he sped down the way, and studied the constellation above the nearest door, further down on the right, briefly thinking and then going through.

I was left here, my mind whirling. Elias Morgan.

He has spoken to you. He seeks your heart. He loves you.

But he spoke in riddles. He had talked to Suffolk. Knew he had owned the House. How had Morgan gotten here, into the maze? Had he crossed through the House? Was there some other way?

Yours Forever

Mentions of Suffolk, of you, of the compass, of the Hounds. He had traveled, and he had studied, clearly. But he walked barefoot, in the maze? Shirtless, with no pack, no supplies? How did he live?

The answer was clear, upon some reflection. He ate what he found, down here in the maze. He lived off the land.

I don't know how.

But that is not the mystery that stays with me.

The only question I care about is his relationship with you. How does he know your heart? He says he speaks to you. Does he? Have you spoken to him?

Does he talk to you now?

He questioned my use of the compass, and studied the constellation before entering the door adjacent to me. Does he know the language of the engravings? He knows something, or thinks he does. Is perhaps he a lucky man, who has survived down here on chance alone?

It is possible, but I dismiss the idea. Anyone who can survive in this place for any length of time has a measure of skill, fortitude, and yes, some luck.

But he knows some things, and probably much more than he let on in this conversation.

Before this litany, I had thought to follow him, to chase after him through the door.

But is it yet another trap? Is he a creation of this place?

It is possible, surely. The powers of the maze and of the many doors are not to be underestimated.

But again, I dismiss the idea.

He is real, and is here in pursuit of your heart. Jealousy spikes in me, even now, well after he's departed, and it will never fully leave me, not with the knowledge of this man, who says he loves you.

But despite his knowledge, and his condescension, he has not freed you. Despite this time spent, he is no closer to you than I. We tread the same ground. And perhaps it is reticence of using the compass that has failed him.

I will do whatever it takes. I will find you. I must sup, and then I will embark through a single door. Then I will sleep.

22

I have made a mistake.

After my last missive, I ate a substantial meal, and then packed my things. I would follow the compass, and go through one more door before setting up camp and sleeping. Without a dependable clock, I must rely on my sense of exhaustion to guide me to rest.

It is a marathon, not a sprint, but after that meal, I saw the end of my rations. I must discover Morgan's source of food and water, or I must turn back and return to the surface. I shudder to think of traveling back through the butcherous cavern, but it is still better than starving.

But now, I hesitate to say I will return at all.

The compass did not lead me down the path taken by Morgan, but I noted the constellation he had entered before I moved on. The compass led me down many hallways, and I marked them as I took any turn, and took note of the starfields.

I passed over two dozen doors before the compass thrummed, at a door with only three stars on its map. I took a deep breath and went through, rolling the dice.

Hot, dry wind greeted me, and a face full of sunlight. The door vanished from my grip, as it always did, but when I turned back to see it, I saw only sand.

A massive dune stood behind me, the dust whipping away in the wind. Sun beat down on me, and sweat beaded on the nape of my neck and then vanished, wicked away by the thirsty sand.

I stood in the midst of a desert. The sun beamed down overhead, massive above me, and dunes towered around me, but none cast a shadow. I looked and saw nothing but sand in all directions.

The door had vanished, either disappearing, or turning to dust, but gone regardless.

Always two doors, Charlie had told me.

The compass did not thrum in my chest.

I must find the other door.

I took off my pack, and grabbed my last spare cloth, soaked it with water, and then tied it around my neck, draping it over my head, a trick I had learned from a friend of father's who had spent time in the French Foreign Legion. It kept the sun from my eyes, and cooled me for the moment. So far, I had held my water supplies at pace with my journey. This desert would test them.

If indeed it was a desert. I would need higher ground, to survey my surroundings.

The dune to my right had the gentlest slope, steep, but climbable, and I scrambled up the side. My feet slid in the sand, all of it incredibly fine, but my hands burned as I clawed at it, to keep from falling. The sun had baked the surface, and it scorched my skin, but I continued to climb. My lungs boiled as I breathed in the fiery air, my heart thudding, but then I reached the top of the dune.

The peak of this dune, but not the highest point. I saw now, dunes that soared even higher, reaching dizzying heights, nearly touching the sun, as far as I could see, into the horizon.

But they were not stagnant, moving like an ocean, a massive dune, miles in the distance, collapsing, crashing, the sand filling a vacuum.

But this desert was more than sand.

The skyscrapers soared in the distance. They reached to the sky and glinted in the light.

I have seen the towering construction of the city, the Empire State Building, the towers.

But these buildings dwarfed them, soaring too high to see, and they swayed in the hot wind. I feared they would topple before my eyes.

But they still stood. I could make out little detail. But I looked in every direction, and they were all that stood. All else was sand, and sun.

The sun was above me, massive. Too big for the sky. Was this our world? Or another?

I could not know, but I lived and breathed. I marked the towers as my destination, and I walked. I stayed on the dune, walking toward the tower, drinking small sips of water when my mouth dried.

As I walked, the towers' size became apparent, as I made little progress, even after seeming hours of trudging through the sifting sands, my ankles and knees aching, my skin scorched from the sun. I had covered myself, with whatever I could, the burn setting in after minutes. I soaked my clothes, and the sun would dry them in mere moments, and I would soak them again. My body had heated, the temperature hotter than I had ever felt.

But the sun was not infinite here. Thank you for that.

It moved in the sky, as large as it was, and shadows were cast, and then I moved to them, and sweet relief swept through me. My body had been fighting a losing battle as its temperature rose and rose, but now it gained back ground. I had approached the towers. I drew nearer to them, I did, but they still loomed over me, far in the distance.

As the sun set, I continued to walk, pushing myself as hard as I could. Walking in the near dark was easier, with the cooler temperatures settling in, and I stepped through shifting dunes until it was too dim to see.

I hope to make the towers tomorrow. I will camp here, and hope the temperatures do not drop too much.

And I hope the second door awaits me there.

23

I buried myself in the sand. It was the only way to survive the night.

The temperature dropped a hundred degrees, with the absence of the sun glaring down. My breath frosted in front of me as I laid in my sleeping bag. I thought I could endure the night, but the numbness of my toes told otherwise.

The sand was my only hope, and I took my camp shovel and dug, digging a well, and then piling the sand on top of me. It retained only slight heat from the day, but it served as an insulator for my body, and I laid that way until the sun rose, with my head and an arm out, both wrapped in the sleeping bag.

I slept fitfully, if at all, but I did not freeze. My stomach growled like a caged beast in the morning, but I ate only enough rations to appease it. I didn't know what lay ahead, aside from raw desert.

At the merest glimpse of light, I unearthed myself, cleaning the sand from crevices, doing my best to remove it all. It would chafe during the day. I packed my things and walked toward the towers.

They soared over me, miles high, higher than possible. I trekked toward them, but they stayed out of my grasp, their height only climbing. There was nothing on Earth built this high, or looked like this. As I drew nearer, I saw the details of the buildings.

They were metal and glass, but nothing I had seen before, the windows dozens of stories tall, the metal beams thin, too thin to support such a great mass. But it held.

Or it had. For the buildings were falling. As I moved closer to them, the sun beating down on me, I stepped on something that was not sand. I stopped for a moment, and brushed away the remnants of sand beneath me, and realized I was stepping on glass, a window of a fallen tower, devoured by the great desert.

I looked down into the glass, through the shadowy portal, and saw nothing inside, too dark to see. The sand had blocked the sun inside. Were there any people in there when it fell? Or were they long dead, too? Was I the lone remaining survivor in this desert world? Had the sun scorched everyone else?

Despite the collapse, the glass remained intact. These materials—they were beyond us.

Or at least beyond us now.

I walked, the sun burning me alive, as it rose above me, dominating the sky. There were no clouds, only the sun and the burning wind. The dunes rose around me and fell, and I walked, taking small sips of water. My water supplies had fallen in this place. The worry nagged inside my mind, but I had to survive this world before I could do anything. I had to find the second door. The towers, they surely held it.

I put down my head and walked, covering myself from the sun above. My mind wandered in the heat, filled with delirium. I thought of the Lover, and his manic smile, and his supposed love for you. I thought of Suffolk. The compass had led me to this door? Had the Architect walked these same steps? And had the Hounds followed him on this trail?

I pushed those questions aside and focused only on you. Your heart, the noble quest, is all that matters. This desert world was just another obstacle between you and me. I thought only of you, even as the sun destroyed me, as the sand scoured my skin, as my lips dried and cracked. You would carry me through all of it.

Then I saw a shadow at my feet, and I looked up and smiled. The tower rose above me, the top soaring out of sight.

And for the first time in this desert world, the compass thrummed in my chest. I smiled, despite myself. The second door lay somewhere inside this tower.

I must merely climb.

I entered the tower, glass doors perpetually open, sand having piled itself high inside the tower's lobby. I had ridden in an elevator in New York City, to the top of a building, and perhaps this would be the same.

I searched for it, moving through the lobby, and found something similar, but the doors were locked shut, and the call button did not work. The building would not have power, so of course the elevator would not work.

I would have to climb. Presumably this building would have steps. It did, next to the elevator, a thin shaft that rose high, steps interweaving on each other. Seeing the steps confirmed this was a building made for humans, the same size and shape. This must be Earth, I puzzled. But which Earth?

I pushed the thought from my mind and climbed.

The temperature inside the tower was mild, a great relief from the sun outside, but the stairs were infinite, and I crossed far more than a thousand. I stopped counting after a while, my legs aching. I paused to take a breath, from time to time, but I did not wait long at any one stop, for as I climbed, the building swayed.

The movement was invisible from the ground below, but in the tower, one felt it move, back and forth, as the hot wind swept across it.

I told myself the building had stood this long. Surely, it would not fall now, of all times. Why would my appearance make the difference in its strength?

And my mind knew that, but the aching feeling in the back of my knees told me otherwise, and I forced myself up the stairs, even as I sweat through my clothes, and my thighs burned with exertion.

Suddenly, I realized I had reached the top, and my heart soared. But the compass still thrummed only slightly, and I went through the swinging door at the top, and I had yet to reach the peak, only the end of this stairwell. I found myself on an open floor, the windows giving me a wide view of this desert world.

And truly, that is what it was. Another two towers stood nearby, still distant, but within sight. But there was nothing else, nothing else but sand and sun.

The desert had swallowed all.

I took in the sight for a moment, catching my breath. Then the building moved again, swaying back and forth.

Was it moving more than it had? No, impossible, but I continued, looking for the next stairwell, and moving on.

I climbed. Climbed for hours, pushing my legs up and up, massaging the knots that formed in my thighs when I reached a landing.

But as I climbed, the compass thrummed more and more. The second door was above, the way out, the way to you.

I climbed, finding the end of the second stairwell, and continuing on to the third. I looked out the windows again, and as high as I was, I saw the tower clearly sway back and forth. Tears formed in my eyes, my stomach churning, but I waited. I needed to know.

The swaying got worse as I watched. I must hurry.

I found the stairwell and climbed quickly, as quickly as my weary bones would carry me. I had slept little the night prior, and the sun had worn me to nothing, but I would surely die inside this tower if it fell.

I climbed.

Step after step, I climbed, pushing myself as hard as I could. The compass shook in my chest, and I told myself it was you, speaking to me through the shaking metal warmed by my blood. You were calling to me, to the second door, to return to the maze, where you were held, somewhere deep inside. I would find you.

The building moved more still, back and forth, back and forth, and I did not know its breaking point, but it felt impossible, the shifting back and forth, an impossible angle for something made of metal and glass. I went up and up, and the compass thrummed even harder through my skin, and my bones vibrated as I drove my quaking legs.

Then I was at the top of the stairs. I pushed through, but I wasn't at the top yet, no, this was the observation level, and I frantically searched around the massive floor, but there was no second door, nowhere to be seen, and I saw an access stairwell, and of course, the door would be as high as possible, on the roof of the building, and I ran through, the tower tilting back and forth, and now I heard the metal straining from the force, and it would snap, and I sprinted up the stairs, and I was back outside, the sun on top of me, I could reach up and touch it, so big, so hot, the wind soaring past me. I was on the peak of the tower, and I could touch the burning sky, and then I heard the building snap, and it tumbled to the side, and I saw the door, standing freely, and I dove for it, and my hand gripped the knob and pushed and I was through.

24

I have eaten the last of my rations and I am still hungry.

I escaped the desert world, back to the hallway maze, emerging from the door in a long stretch of barren hallway, with no doors in sight aside from the one I just emerged from.

After sending my last missive, I spent a time recovering from my journey through the desert. I laid down and slept. I do not know how long, but I was ravenously hungry when I awoke, and thirsty as sin, and I ate what remained of my rations. Not that I stuffed myself—I merely ate what I had left, which was not plenty.

I'm doing better with water, with perhaps a quarter of my total stock remaining. I am not desperate yet, not completely, not with my stock of water, but I must search for food. I do not wish to return to the surface, to the House. I get closer to you with every set of doors, and I cannot reset my progress.

But I cannot survive another trek through the desert. If I am to return, it must be through other means.

The rations were not enough to stave off my hunger. It still lurks there, at the edge of my feeling, and soon, it will return full force and I will have nothing for it but water.

But the Lover has remained, and he carries nothing but that knife. He lives off the land, he must, or he has set up a base of sorts, somewhere, in a room that is sustainable, with access to supplies. I should have followed him and asked him how he survived, but there was too much anger in me, at his impertinence and impropriety. I know I must divorce my emotions from my survival, remove them from the equation, all in pursuit of rescuing you, but I find it difficult when the man talks so closely of you, when it's impossible he knows you like I know you. How could he? How could he?

But after taking a long period of rest and recovery from the desert world, I climbed back up on my aching legs and walked the hallways, waiting for the resonant hum of the compass as it shook in my chest, telling me I was close to the next path, the next door that would lead me to you.

But I found nothing.

Not nothing, truly. I found more doors, and many rights and lefts and intersecting hallways, and I marked each one with chalk, systemically avoiding doubling back, wandering the wooden floors, paying close attention to the compass, waiting for it to thrum, where I could dial in the location of my next passage.

Truth be told, I did more than that. I also listened for the bare stamping of feet, of Morgan, the Lover, the hedonist. I half-dreaded seeing him again, but I still needed him. He had the knowledge of this place, and I would be remiss if I did not study when I had the opportunity. I did not want to face his smell, his filth, and his wavering smile, but if he knew the source of supplies, I must sup with him, metaphorically, of course.

But I heard him not, nor smelled his stink, nor saw no sign of him. Or anything else, for that matter. The isolation of the maze felt particularly acute after the torture of the desert world and its complete loneliness.

But I continued on, marking every door I crossed, taking each constellation down in my notebook. I still had found no similarities in the rooms I had visited and their coordinates marked on the engravings above their doors. If indeed that's what they were. If I could parse them, would they tell me something more? Would they tell me the danger contained within, or their proximity to you? Or if there was food and water inside?

But if there were six billion rooms, I do not know how I would find any conclusions. The Architect had created a place that could not be cataloged or studied. It could only be delved.

After many hours, the compass finally hummed in my chest, and as I slowly moved, it shook harder and harder, my heartbeat thumping in kind.

Yours Forever

I finally found the door, which had all but one star lit on its engraving. I had yet to see a door with that many stars lit, and I questioned if it meant something.

Before I entered, I paused, to speak to you. I wanted to transmit something to mark my progress. The desert world made it clear any door could mark my end. That I will send you a transmission, and it will not be clear until afterward it was my final missive. And so I try to send them often.

But I do not believe it so in my heart. I believe I will open this door, and find the other side, and move forward, follow the compass, and recover your heart. I believe it deeply. There isn't a possibility of failure, not if I am true to my quest and to your intent. Fate and I are intertwined, just as I am with you. I am destined to be your knight, your savior.

Through this door, and onward.

25

I have emerged from the room, but I truly do not know what I saw inside.

As soon as I entered, there was no space, not that I could perceive. I was thrown, moving quickly, my body bombarded by sensations, overwhelmed by feelings. I could not get my bearings, no landmarks to mark, no second door to find. It was only a wash of color and sound, of smell and taste that filled my mouth and tongue, of everything all at once.

Then I stood in a city, but my feet did not touch the ground. I was there but not, and I watched the people, moving through their lives, walking down the street. They were all faceless, all nameless, and I reached for one as we crossed, but my hand passed through their form, and all I heard was the noise of the city, of the cars, the trains, the people.

And then there was an enormous clap, and I looked to the sky, and saw a light, brighter than bright, the light building, and building, and building, impossible, but it built still.

I was transfixed, unable to move, helpless to look away, powerless to shut my own eyes, even as I was blinded, and more than the light it built, but a building wave of destruction roared out from the light, crashing, endless crashing, louder than the Dweller's ocean, waves of white hot explosion roaring toward me, buildings disappearing in front of me.

My vision was filled with orange-white fire, and it was a bomb, too large to exist, too powerful for human possibility, but it cascaded outward, destroying everything in its path. The townspeople vanished in its trail, simply disappearing, the nameless and faceless now formless, and I tried to run, to duck, to hide, but I was immobile, and the destruction passed through me, but I was unphased.

The wave cascaded outward past me, and I heard the catastrophe. All I tasted and smelled was ash and dust, the city laid bare.

A cloud grew in front of me, towering, like the towers of the great desert, an aftermath too large to comprehend. I screamed, I screamed, and the roaring noise of destruction pushed me through into a realm of white and swirling black, a field of noise that trapped me, surrounded me.

High pitched and modulating, the white noise encompassed me, the landscape now nothing but a field of chaos. I tried to breathe, but all I breathed was the sound, my body had become it now, and it ripped through me, where was I? Who was I? Impossible to tell, overwhelmed by sound and noise, and then the sound changed, my vision not filled by images, my vision *was* images. A man at a podium, in a suit, he was the President, I knew he was, but I did not recognize him, and he declared victory, victory over what I didn't know but the image switched, no context, a flooded image of a man at a desk, speaking over the image of bombs dropping, of fire and death, of bombed-out buildings, who was this man, what was this war, but then it changed again, image after image, of products I didn't recognize, of cans and cartons of cigarettes, of women wearing nothing, of impossible vehicles and imaginary sports.

My mind stared, attempting to parse what I saw, but it was too much, too fast, the images not slowing down but accelerating, faster than I could see, the sounds and colors too much, impossible. I begged, I pleaded, please, please, stop, stop, slow, slow.

But the culture did not slow, but sped even faster, and I breathed it in, the images and sound, and I was it, nothing but data. I had become one with this swarming cloud of steam, and I was filled with oppressive hate.

Not one, not dozens, not thousands, but millions of thoughts and feelings, flooding my mind, hateful, blind rage, screaming into my psyche about failure, about kindness, about belief, and they spun through faster than I could think, punctuated by gunfire. I tasted the smoke in my mouth, the taste of fire and destruction, of the world burning, of the mushroom clouds, of the static white noise, of the oppressive hate, and that's all we were, that's all we would become.

I was shown this and a thousand other things, all in the blink of an eye, but none of it was real, not yet, the sense of things yet to come, of scale in time that shattered me, and I was trapped there, bombarded with it, my eyes, my nose, my ears, my throat, all open, and I was filled, the room pouring every sensation inside of me, the history of the world, behind and ahead, deep into my bowels, filling every cavity, and tears flowed from me, sadness, anger, ecstasy filling me all at once, and my brain burned at the sheer holy terror.

I would have begged for it to stop, but I had no breath, no tongue, no mouth to speak with, I was the change, I was the history, I was data, but then it ended, and I was spat out of the second door like Jonah from his great whale, cast back into the utter silence of the hallways.

I laid on the wooden floor, and I wept, crying, crying, until the memories and sensations bled from my mind, evaporating into the ether, as quickly as they had entered, leaving me empty.

Are you showing me these things, Beloved?

Or is it the maze, trying to trick me?

What is the purpose?

What is the plan?

26

I have seen a ghost.

I met Suffolk. I spoke to him. He did not know me, did not recognize me.

But he is dead, he cannot be. I saw him dead. The Hounds ripped him apart. I took the compass from his chest and placed it in mine. He cannot be, he cannot.

And it was not an imitation, as far as I could tell, not a duplicate. He was the man in the pictures in the House above, down to the slight mustache, and the striking eyes that will not maintain eye contact, no matter his confidence or station.

I was recovering from the room, the room of time and place, and I heard the footsteps, heard someone approaching, and I readied myself, my hand drawing my pistol, but it was not Morgan that appeared, not the damned Hedonist, but Suffolk, the Architect appearing from around a corner. He was shocked at my appearance, and put his hands up in reaction to my gun.

"Please, do not shoot me," he said. "I mean you no harm."

I held the pistol still, staring at him, disbelieving.

"Are you James Suffolk?" I asked, finally finding my voice.

"Y—yes," he answered. "Who—who are you?"

"I am Henry," I said, and I lowered my aim. I do not know why. He was the enemy. He was the man who imprisoned you. Or is the man who imprisoned you. All tense applies, as he exists both in the present and only in the past. I should have shot him dead, and or at least drove him into a corner, and interrogated him until he surrendered your location.

But instead, I lowered my pistol and holstered it.

"I did not expect to see anyone this far in the maze," he said, approaching slowly. "I have not met you, have I?"

"We haven't met," I said, not lying. "I only know of you."

"Ah, yes," he said, his eyes darting away from mine. "My name tends to travel ahead of me, regardless of my intent." He looked at a watch. "I have the time. May I sit?"

It seemed a foolish notion, for him to ask permission of me, to sit in a place he built, or at least ordained. But I nodded all the same. I struck the thought in my head, that I must ask him. Ask him where you are. Here is my chance. I must not let it pass.

He sat down, leaning back against the wooden wall, pulling his legs up tight to his chest. His meager pack sat next to him.

"How are you faring?" he asked.

"I have made it this far," I said, unsure of how to answer. I was not dead, torn apart by the Hounds. I was not stricken by an infinite beach. I was alive, surviving the great desert, the whirlwind of sensation, the lake of blood. I did not say that.

"Yes, it is as good a metric as any," he said. "Survival. It took me quite a time to find my footing in that regard. I nearly starved a half dozen times before I found a system that works."

"And what is that?" I asked. "If you're willing to share."

"Of course," he said. "We are all friends here." He smiled, an uneasy smile. Did he believe that? "There are certain doors that lead to plenty, oases in the desert, so to speak."

"Do not speak of deserts."

"Ah, yes," he said. "You have been through the sand. A terrible time. Do you have a notebook?" He stared at me, and I met his eyes. There was no ill will there. I nodded. "May I see it?"

I reached into my pack and pulled it out, and handed it over. He pulled a pen from a side pouch and flipped to a fresh page, scribbling something. "Here." He handed it back.

I grabbed my book and looked at his work. It was coordinates, with some written directions.

"If you have the coordinate of the desert," he said. "Find that door, just beyond it. It will take you to the same place, without the trek. It only requires handing over some personal knowledge, but requires no bloodshed or exertion. It is worth the exchange."

I nodded. "Thank you," I said. Why does he help me?

"Of course," he said. He sighed. "Did the tower fall for you as well?"

I hesitated. "Yes," I said, finally. "Are you saying the same happened to you? A falling tower with the door at the peak?"

"Yes," he said. "It is a thing you learn here. Cycles. Many cycles."

I nodded, but said nothing else. "How did you learn of this shortcut?"

"Experience."

"Just that? Simple trial and error?" I asked. "I thought—"

"You thought what?"

"It is what brought me here," I said. "I studied your work. I thought you had constructed this."

"No," he said. "I have not."

"But your work, it is all over the House," I said. "It is through the House that I found the maze."

"What house?" he asked. I studied his face, but he betrayed no deception. I waited, but he just stared. Either he was the best liar on two feet, or it was the truth. "I did not enter through a house. The maze was through the Obelisk." He returned the same stare. "You entered a different way."

"I did," I said. "Down a thousand steps."

"Yes," said Suffolk. "The same thousand steps, then. But a different path." I looked at him, and he had looked away, his eyes thoughtful. I realized Suffolk looked young, younger than his pictures. His face was overgrown with stubble, and his hair was messy and disheveled, which hid his age. But he was young, younger than me, barely a grown man. The Suffolk I had seen dead had been middle-aged, most likely in his fifties.

Cycles, indeed.

"What are you in search of?" I asked.

His eyes returned to mine. He paused.

"Her," he said. "It is what we all pursue, is it not?"

My heart thudded dully. "Yes," I said, finally. "It is. You have not—"

"Been successful?" he finished. "No. Our circumstances would be much different if I had been. I have been thwarted many times. There is a sense that you are close, that you approach her. I have felt her, the power of her, making my bones ache, filling something deep within me—" He stopped himself. "But then, an obstacle appears. The maze fights, tooth and nail, and shifts, moves, and what I thought was the final door, the door that leads to her, it moves, it travels, and I am alone, in this maze, to retrace my steps back to supplies, to fight through hell, back and forth."

"How do you know where she is? How do you navigate?" I asked. "I have attempted to study the coordinates, the engravings, but it has proven fruitless thus far."

He shook his head. "I did the same, for quite a while. For some time, I was sure that the more stars, the more likely it would lead to her, no matter their orientation. But over time, that theory was proven wrong. No, finding any correlation or causation in the starfield has been a fool's errand. Now, I trust my heart."

"And that has worked?"

"It has gotten me close, several times," he said. "Alongside taking careful notes, of course. My heart does not preclude using my research and study. I find thoroughfares of rooms that require little, or even a bounty."

"But the shifting—"

"Yes," he said. "It can make things difficult. But over time, you have a sense of when and how the maze will change. And I adjust to its movements. It is utterly frustrating, but there is no other way to her."

I nodded. He was not lying. My assumptions—I must question everything. Things were not as they seemed.

"How are your supplies?" he asked.

I answered honestly. "Out of rations. A small amount of water."

He nodded and reached into his pack. He handed me a paper-wrapped bundle and a canteen. The canteen was heavy, full.

"This will help," he said. "If only until you find some supplies."

"I cannot—"

"Please," he said. "I would have killed for this help when I began. Take it. Please."

I pursed my lips, and then nodded, accepting his gift, stowing them in my bag. My stomach grumbled again at the thought of food.

He looked at his watch. "I must get moving." He paused, and then got up, grabbing his pack. "Would you—would you like to travel together?

Even for a time?"

The question was absurd. I could not travel with the enemy. But was he an enemy? He had not captured you, had not imprisoned you. He was on the same search as me. He was not a deviant, like the Lover.

I considered it. But I couldn't. This was my journey, my quest. I could not share you, no matter the temperament.

"I cannot," I said. "I must go alone."

"I understand," he said. "I hope to see you again. Good luck. Follow your heart to her. It is the best judgment I can find. Goodbye."

"Goodbye," I said, and he was off, walking past me, without looking back.

My heart trembled, and I squeezed my hands together, to keep them from shaking. The ghost of the Architect. It was an impossible thing, but I had met him, spoke to him. And he searched for you. Everything he said had answered a question, and then asked another. I could not puzzle it now. I must go to my notes.

He said to follow my heart. That it would not lead me astray. Yet it is his compass I carry inside me. The Architect did not trust his heart. He trusted the machine.

Did it lead to his death?

Cycles. Cycles, indeed.

27

It cannot be coincidence. If this maze truly holds six billion rooms—the realm of possibility that puts me, and a Suffolk, but then again, and then— I am ahead of myself. I had scarcely finished my conversation with Suffolk. He had given me some rations, as well as some water. He moved on, and walked away, down a hallway.

I rested more, thinking through my conversation with the young Suffolk. I would ponder it more, but I could not allow the conversation to stifle my journey deeper into the maze, and closer to you.

I forced my weary legs up, and carried my bag, and explored back how Suffolk had come. I remembered Suffolk's words, of trusting his heart. My heart had led me to the Hounds, and near death.

So instead, I waited for the thrum of the compass in my chest, my mechanical heart leading me instead.

I walked down hallways, marking them as I turned, waiting for the vibration in my chest, the sensation that was becoming familiar, a sign of progress, a feeling I had once found completely alien, slowly feeling welcome.

But there was no vibration. I wandered for a while, marking every perimeter of every portion of the maze, every passing door. I still marked their constellation. I had not abandoned the idea I could catalog them and find a system that would allow me to mark their passage. While I still had room in my notebook, I would notate their coordinates.

I do not know how long I wandered, but the compass did not shake before I heard more footsteps echoing back to me from somewhere ahead.

It could not be Suffolk, could it? No. He had traveled back, behind me. Not unless he had looped around. I paused, and crept slowly, keeping my hand close to my pistol, and my body close to the wall.

The footsteps echoed, and I located the steps, triangulated their position, and I realized they came from the hallway straight ahead, and from the left, and I tucked in a hallway, and waited. Waited to see who else stalked the halls.

The footsteps came quickly, faster than a walk, a steady jog, as the steps hit the wooden floor. They were running.

What were they running from?

I waited, and he came around the corner, considering which direction to go, and I stared.

I studied them, my eyes reading their face, distant but not too distant, and I recognized him. I had seen it three times now, once above, in the House, in the many photographs.

The second, down below, still, his throat and body torn apart by the unseeable fangs of the Hounds.

And third, only moments ago, a calm, youthful face, that offered advice and spare rations.

It was Suffolk, again. Impossible, all impossible. But this Suffolk was older, similar to the corpse which I had pried the compass from. He was harried, and he turned toward me, and I backed down the corridor, quiet on my feet, and retreated, tucking into the next closest perpendicular hallway. I peered out with an eye alone, waiting for him to pass, and he did, only glancing down my direction before jogging ahead. The sound of his breath filled the passageway. He had been running for a while, his skin shining, but then he was gone, sprinting past, heading the same direction he had just gone.

But not the same Suffolk. A difference of years between them. What had happened in that time?

I needed to know. I had spoken to Suffolk. To get the full picture, I must speak to the Architect.

I left my hiding place, following him, hurrying. I did not hide my footsteps, impossible at a jogging speed. I would talk to the Architect, and find out what his role in all of this was.

I heard him ahead of me, his footfalls pounding on the wooden floors, and I followed him as best as I could, his noises echoing back to me, and past the twists and turns, back past the exit to the room of sounds and time, and kept moving.

But something was wrong. I had a feeling, on the brink of perceiving something, when arms wrapped around me, and pulled me aside, down a side hallway, and I resisted but I was not strong enough, not now, not after days down here, and maybe never, and the arms dragged me through a door, and dumped me on the ground of a place I didn't know.

I looked up to see Morgan, bare-chested, for once not smiling. He stood in front of the closed door, looking at me, his eyes staring at me with wild concern.

"What are you doing? Where are we—"

"Oh, pup," he said. "You seemed smarter."

"I was going to speak to him! To the Architect, and you dragged me away, like a criminal, like some rogue, to some room—"

"This is a safe place," he said. "Safe enough. Not a locked room—" He stopped, scanning past me. "—no immediate danger. I didn't think there would be. We can head back out in a few minutes." He smiled to himself, and then it stayed, the contracting and expanding grin.

I looked back, behind me, picking myself off the floor, and we stood inside a cave, the exit within sight, the view only sky. The whistling of the wind blew past me, and carried a slight salt and smoky air. But Morgan was right. There was no danger, not readily apparent.

"That still does not excuse dragging me away—"

"Hush, pup," he said. "What do you think was chasing Suffolk?"

I stopped, back to staring at him. I said nothing.

"Don't play dumb," he said. "You know the answer. You've seen the work."

"The Hounds," I said, realizations blossoming.

"Yes," he said. He pointed to his skull. "You felt them, in here, a tingle on the brain. A sense of a sense. If you feel it again, you can identify it. But another moment, and they would have been in sight, and you would be a target."

"They're after Suffolk," I said. "They kill him."

"They will," said Morgan. "He has some time." He smiled wider. "Or none at all."

"I met him," I said. "A young man."

"Ah, yes," said Morgan. "He's the nice one. We supped, once upon a time. But we went our separate ways. He leaves the maze, disappears for a time. When he returns, he is older—and darker. With the Hounds in pursuit."

"Did he see them down here?"

"I'd be willing to wager," he said. "Unfortunately, I'm out of greenbacks. You'll have to take my word."

"You saved my life," I said, quietly.

He nodded. "I will take credit, if you will give it."

"Why?"

He smiled wide. "Oh, pup. She wants you to live. And I am not one to deny her. Maybe you will be the one. Not if I can help it, of course, but you may."

"You speak to her," I said. His previous boast was not an empty claim.

"Yes," he said. "Almost every day, I send a missive, as I'm certain you do as well. There was a fallow period, once—"

He trailed off. And his smile almost vanished. But then it returned.

"—But it ended. I found the pull again, and I followed it back to my faith. And if the Beautiful wants you to live, then I follow her beckon."

Beautiful? I stared at him, bare-chested, his hirsute mustache hanging over his massive smile. His musk mixed with the smoky salt air and floated through my nostrils. They rankled, but my reaction was tempered, tempered by my savior.

He followed you. You compelled him to save me. Was it true? I did not want to owe this man my life, but he had saved me from the Hounds, which would be a certain death, sometime in the far future.

"You said this room features unlocked doors. How do you know that?"

"A long worth of trial and error," he said. He eyed me, in the dim light of the cave. "Let me see your notebook."

I hesitated, and then removed my pack and pulled my notebook from it. I held it out to him. He took it, his fingers grazing mine, sharing small contact. His skin was a shark's, rough friction.

He opened, flipping to a random scribbling of a coordinate. He pointed at the lowest void.

"The thirteenth," he said. "If it is lit, then the door will be locked, or moved. No return journey, until you reach the other side, and go back through. Not helpful, if you're looking for a brief reprieve, or a quick cut."

"The others?" I asked.

He closed my book and handed it back to me, our fingers grazing again. "That would be telling."

"You save my life, but deny me knowledge?"

"She hasn't told me to share, and so I will be the stinge," he said, smiling at me. "And I intend to free my lady. It is what we all want. Why we all came."

My earlier jealousy rose again. How dare he.

"Oh, oh no. The rose in your cheeks, that fire in your belly. It is why she likes you. Well, I hope she doesn't expect me to go easy on you."

And then he winked, and went back out of the door we had entered through.

28

I did not follow Morgan. I needed to think, and if he was correct, this was a safe place to do so.

I took a glance out the mouth of the cave. From my initial vantage point, only the sky was visible, but as I approached the exit, I saw a more complete picture.

The cave mouth overlooked a winding cliff-side path that led down hundreds of feet to a dense arboreal forest. Treetops were only visible from up above, the timber thick. I saw no break in the trees.

The wind whistled past me, the smell of minerals wafting through, but nothing else. I waited, pausing. Distant thumps reached my ears, the sound of something heavy, stepping.

Safe enough, Morgan had said. Perhaps in this cave mouth. The massive source of those steps might beg to differ, if I was to embark down below. But the compass hadn't led me here. I would not explore, despite my curiosity in what the source of those heavy footfalls was.

Too much had happened too quickly. I must take some time to process. I cannot continue on with my journey with half-formed theories. If I am to make a choice, I must have a reasoning.

Suffolk, the Architect, is dead. His body ripped and torn by the Hounds. His compass, pulled from his chest, now inside mine.

Suffolk, the young man, still explores the maze. He has learned some lessons. He is generous with his supplies, and with his knowledge. He wanders in search of you. Like we all are. He entered through an obelisk, and knows nothing of the House. He speaks of cycles.

The Architect, the elder, runs through the maze, pursued by the Hounds. He is run ragged. He has returned to the maze below, after a time away. He will die.

A timeline of his life, lain before me, and in the House above. He designed the House, building it from the ground up.

I had assumed the maze below was his work as well. Had assumed too much. Has assumed he had imprisoned your heart, deep inside.

The maze is not Suffolk's work. That is to be sure.

All my research had mentioned him obliquely, always connected to you, and your vacant organ. Never was he explicitly guilty. But the connection and his obsession were obvious.

But he had been searching, just like me. The younger Suffolk had searched for a time, and at some point, abandoned it. He had returned to the quest, an older man. Hunted. Had built the House, and had tethered the maze to it.

To bring you closer? I do not know. Some questions can only be asked of the elder, and he cannot answer. Truly, any contact with him would risk contact with the Hounds. Despite my actions, I have no death wish.

Morgan knows of the Suffolks. Knows more than he lets loose, and is combative, aggressive.

But he also saved my life. Under your orders, he said. Speaks of your affection for me. But it is a competition to him. He wants to be the one that rescues you. Who pulls you from this wicked trap.

Does he speak to you? He knows of you, calls you Beautiful. Or is he suffering a multitude of delusions?

Am I?

Suffolk speaks of freeing you. Says the many here have come for you. Another assumption, broken. The many. How many? How many have fallen, broken in the maze, destroyed by entering an unknown door?

How many are still inside?

It still feels no coincidence I have seen Suffolk, or Morgan himself. Are you orchestrating? Are you using your influence to guide us together?

How far does your influence lie? How much can you pull without your beating heart?

I struggle with it all. If the numbers are true, and there are so many doors, how can I possibly find the right one? Will this compass truly guide my path? Is it blasphemous to rely on it? Or does the end justify the means?

But I submit only for the thought. For if I am to pause and stop at every moment of existentialism, I would be rooted to the spot, a petrified gargoyle of justification and fate, guarding this place for all eternity, waiting for the impossible to become the obvious.

It is a fool's thought, to wait to know something one cannot know. One must surrender one's self to something greater. To the massive, to the colossal.

And so I surrender to you.

If Morgan's truth about the stars is that, then I now have a space for solace and sanctuary, provided I find the right door at the right time.

I must avoid the elder Suffolk, for with him comes the Hounds.

Morgan is an enigma. He wants you for himself, but still follows you.

The younger Suffolk will help.

If I see him again.

I will run short on food and water. I must find a source. I will trust the compass to lead me. I follow it.

I follow you.

29

I have tread on a god, Beloved.

I left the cave shortly after my last missive. The hallways were quiet, with no evidence of Suffolk or Morgan. Or the Hounds.

I pieced together my previous path. Away from the door of time and space. I have removed my watch, for any sense of real time is gone. I thought I could trust my hunger, but even that had been distorted by the maze.

The only true marker is my progress toward you.

I crossed a great distance in the maze. I counted four hundred doors in my travel today, waiting for the compass to vibrate, to alert me to proximity. I marked my progress with the chalk. The piece I used had worn down to a nub, and then gone, but I carried many pieces, enough to last for an eternity.

But I traveled far, farther through the maze between doors than I ever had. The compass had been quiet.

Frankly, I worried. Would it remain quiet? Had this same issue plagued Suffolk, and lost him to the Hounds? How could none of these doors bring me closer to you?

I paused, eating half a ration, as much as I dare before I fully resupplied, and drinking only sips of water. It was enough to carry me. I would save the remainder.

Shortly after my rest, the compass softly thrummed, and my heart rejoiced. The anxious ache inside me eased, just a portion, enough to breathe, and followed the compass's shaking, until it threatened to pull itself from my chest.

A door. Its thirteenth void was marked, and so in Morgan's logic, it was safe to enter and exit, without recourse.

I entered and was presented with a funerary landscape.

It left me breathless.

It took me a few moments to realize what I saw and where I stood.

Stretched out before me was the body of a massive being, two arms, two legs, humanoid, although I could not see its face, not from my vantage point. I saw little of the detail of its body, for it was much too large, and much too far away.

I stood on the crest of its foot, its boot tip behind me, me a Lilliputian to the massive creature. Was it a boot? I do not know, but I did not stand on its flesh, but some sort of material. Its legs stretched out in front of me, and they were similarly clothed, in some sort of hard substance. Although perhaps this creature was not made from flesh at all.

I looked back, and the door still stood there, ready for my ingress, if needed. But there was no danger here, none I saw, aside from perhaps falling from the body of this god.

For that is what it was, no matter how my mind framed it. I looked out, away from the body, and I saw a planet, saw a landscape, far, far down. I saw no details, but I saw movement. I saw towns, and cities, and even electric lights. I saw the movement of life and death, all overshadowed by the still frame of the god. And perhaps this god did not create this place, but its power and might guaranteed it dominance and sovereign. With a single step, it could crush any of the life that had sprung up in its shadow.

Had it not died, time and entropy a more powerful force than it. And it was dead, no breath emerging from its massive form, no movement, not even a sleepful shudder.

A sun beamed down from above, but the weather was temperate.

My travel seemed clear. Traverse the god ahead, and so I walked, testing my footsteps on the great creature. It was solid, my boots finding firm footing beneath me, the massive thing with no fragile give.

I walked, making slow progress. The size of the god was not apparent, the scale too large. I could not understand such a thing, just as I could not see the scope of a mountain in my mind. But it was a mountain I hiked, for if I fell from one of its cliffs, I would not survive, my body broken by the long fall, down into the society that lived in its view.

I walked, keeping my eyes on my feet, and letting my mind wander. It was a pleasant journey, one not beset by Hounds or terrible horrors. A breeze blew through, a cool, dry wind, and I stopped, and closed my eyes, and let it enrich my spirit. There would be darkness ahead, surely, as there was behind. But I held the lovely breeze, and distilled it in my mind, tying it to thoughts of you. You were at the end of this. I could not lose sight.

I hiked more, moving onto the god's thick leg, the outer hard material and dark purple, leaving the black of its boot behind. I walked until my stomach growled deep inside me, and I forced myself farther. I had made efforts to stretch my meager rations, and this was another attempt at that. I walked until I observed evidence of its torso in the far distance, and then I allowed myself a ration. The donation by young Suffolk had helped, but I saw the end of my food supplies again. I would need to find more, and this god was no garden.

I ate a half ration, enough to quiet my hunger, and moved again, forcing myself forward. This world's sun had withdrawn, setting on the other side of the god, and darkness filled the world below. I walked, making it to the hip of the deity, even as I scarcely saw my own feet. I looked back, and could not make out the god's feet either.

In the dark, we both disappear.

I wanted to continue, but I would not risk a deadly fall. I stopped and set up a primitive camp. Tomorrow I see the face of a god.

30

I have seen the face of a god, Beloved, but more than that, as well.

I have seen his innards.

The rising sun woke me, bright in my eyes, and I wasted no time, only drinking a slight amount of water, and eating nothing. My rations would not last me over two more days. I must stretch them to their limits. Although my experience today challenged that notion.

I started my god hike, hoping to summit its head before the sunset. I would hope to find the second door there and continue back into the maze.

But I was interrupted by activity and movement. I saw it in the distance, as I moved toward the giant's torso. It had been obscured by the darkness of the night before, but now the activity was impossible to miss. The god's body was not alone. Something had been constructed on it, attached to it. I saw distant figures, darkly moving over the form, through and across the constructions.

My thoughts of peace from the day prior had been errant. I had wanted to encounter none of the locals, but it seemed an impossibility if I was to continue further. I walked, keeping my head up, watching as the sight became clear as I approached.

It was scaffolding.

The figures climbed up and down the wooden ladders and across the boards. They had built miles of it, covering the torso of the god. Dozens, no, hundreds of them, they climbed up and down, long lines of them, packages, bags, something, strapped to their backs.

I approached, watching them work. What were they ferrying? Why did they scramble?

I got closer, waiting for them to spot me, to call me out, but if they saw me, they said nothing, did nothing but continue their toil. And toil it was, as I came closer, at the edge of their construction, on the border of their scaffolding. I saw their work, saw their great effort. They were miners, of a sort. Or perhaps butcher was a better label. But what is the difference? They harvested, either stone or meat.

The alien locals had carved a hole into the torso of the great being, of the corpse of the monolithic god. They had cut through its lavender shell, armor, or whatever it may be, and then burrowed into its flesh, a light gray skin that covered inky black innards. How long had they operated on the creature I do not know, but they now worked in a massive hole inside the god, scaffolding built all around the crevice, with more ladders extending down into its dark organs.

They climbed down inside, their hands and feet coated in black viscera, and climbed back out, dark bundles strapped to their backs, bound to them with coils of stained rope. Back and forth they climbed, down into the god and then out again, scurrying over its body, and then down to the surface, down hundreds more feet of ladders, down to the normal world of life and death.

But what did they carry?

And would they be friendly to me?

I walked closer, stepping foot onto their extensive scaffolding, made from a wood I could not identify. I was within a hundred feet of them, the stream of locals, and I saw them now, saw them up close.

They were not human. Their skin was the same gray as the god that lay below us, and their stained hands bore four fingers instead of five. They had no noses, only a small mouth, and enormous eyes, with black pupils that dominated them. The tops of their heads were not covered in hair, but in semi-luminescent scales, scattered in color and ornamentation. Had they come from the sea?

I was in plain sight now, but still they hurried past, only glancing at me.

Their work consumed them, and despite being a foreigner to them, they had little concern for me. Had they seen others traveling between the two doors?

Despite my curiosity, this was a diversion. The key to you did not lay in this world, and I would continue through to return to the maze. I would need to thread their work-line, and I paused, waiting for a gap in the locals as they marched to and fro, from the guts of the god back to their city below.

There was a small gap, and I did not hesitate, hurrying through their line, to not disrupt their efforts. I hurried, and succeeded, finding myself on the other side, the workers continuing their haul.

I looked back, once, but then returned forward, hiking toward the head, and the second door.

"Anargh!" yelled a voice, the first I had heard from the locals, and it turned my vision toward it, and one of them had broken from their ranks, and came toward me, frantically. My hand went to my pistol, but I realized there was no need. The creature was not aggressive. Indeed, it approached with its hands up, cradling something. I realized it was making an offering to me. It was a gift.

It approached, now close to me. The scales on its head were shaped like a spade, fluorescing in a rainbow as the sun glinted off. The creature was shorter than me, only five feet tall. Its massive eyes considered me. It gestured its open hands toward me, pleading with me to take its gifts.

I examined it and realized quickly what it was. It was the fruits of their labor, the deep toil of their work inside the body of the god.

It offered a substantial cut of the god's flesh, bleeding black blood. The steak was hefty, a prime gift, on top of a waxy paper which protected the meat once wrapped. The smell was overpowering, of vinegar and ammonia, the chemical smell of an apothecary and toxic gas, of a trench of the Great War.

I was struck by twinned desires then, of disgust and desire, this awful flesh an unholy thing, the butchered meat of a dead god, of a corpse not meant for mortal hands to dissect, of the ghastly smell warning of a deadly poison.

But something else reached out to me, pulling me toward the meat. Of an impossible, primal urge, trapped inside of man since Adam, of consuming the holy, of elevating oneself to the realm of deity. Something inside screamed for the flesh.

"Anargh! Anargh!" repeated the creature. It pushed the gift toward me, and I saw other faces of the locals turn toward us, staring with wide eyes, and I could not offend, and I took the gift from it, gently cradling.

"Anargh!" it yelled a final time, and then closed the waxy paper around the steak in my hands, folding and bundling, tucking the paper around it, and pushing toward me. Its dry and scaly skin touched mine, feeling like a snake, and then it was gone, returning to work, to harvest more unholy and forbidden flesh.

The faces of the others had returned to their work as well, leaving me alone. I took the steak and tucked it into my bag. The wax paper had sealed it well, and I would consider it further later.

The sun was still in the sky, and I returned to my hike, leaving the locals and their butchery behind me. The dry wind hit me once again, but I could not return to my reverie from the day prior. I continued my long walk, the sun trailing through the sky, the only passage of time I could trust.

It was nearing dark again when I saw the second door. It stood on the chin of the god. It was distant, and I moved quickly now, pushing toward it. My stomach grumbled. I had not eaten all day, but I ignored it, continuing my trek.

A ladder stood between the chest of the god and its chin, but it was not a ladder of the locals, but a ladder of my Earth. Perhaps the young Suffolk had left it here. It looked to be of his craftsmanship. I did not tarry to examine it, climbing in the waning light. Hand over hand I climbed, ascending to the god's face.

The door stood only twenty feet away, and I approached it. I could have opened it, and gone through, but the limits on my curiosity are finite.

Instead, I walked past it for a moment, and took in the face of this god.

I stared at it, and then returned to the door, walking through it, returning to the maze.

I made camp and ate as little ration as I could. I would need to find food, surely.

I did not open the gift from the alien local, the prime cut of their departed god.

I will sleep now, and speak again tomorrow.

Its face was theirs.

Its face was theirs.

31

I am out of rations, and there is no younger Suffolk here to help.

After leaving the dead god, I have searched for a source of replacement rations. Both Suffolk and Morgan have survived on food from the maze, but I have found nothing that would replenish my supplies.

Using Morgan's information, I have peeked inside any door that promises an easy and safe return, but in none of them have I found any food, at least none within a reasonable distance or with ease of access. Perhaps I would find some with some amount of exploration, but my body has finite resources, and I must account for any measure of exertion. I cannot afford a high cost without surety of finding replenishment.

I've looked into several dozen doors, none bearing any fruit. Some have been portals into other worlds, places unrecognizable to my human eyes, to rooms and homes on my Earth, but none I have been comfortable exploring.

Even this mild activity leaves me exhausted, and I've slept more and more. My hunger has been the only reliable timekeeping in the maze, but now my clock is always running, my stomach gnawing at me endlessly, aching for want of some kind of subsistence. I sip at water, and it delays the ache, or pushes it away, but it will also not last. And when I have run dry of water, it will be the end of me.

I have searched and searched, ignoring the thrumming of the compass as it neared and then identified the next door in my journey to you. This constellation was not marked with the safe coordinate, and the door would vanish when I went through. And what if it was another desert? Another trek through a barren landscape? I would perish before I reached the other side.

And I will not die. My mission is paramount, my quest absolute, and anything besides your rescue is inexcusable.

I did not want to do it.

But I had pushed my hunger to its furthest bounds. I was fighting off weakness, and your heart is the end, whatever the means.

I had not touched the meat from the dead god, although its chemical smell had infiltrated the rest of my things, emanating from its wax paper bounds. I had pushed it aside every time I reached for a ration that was not there, as I have searched for some sort of sustenance. But it is all I have.

I did not want to eat it, Beloved.

I tried to start a fire with the meager things I had. I had matches, but little fuel, and I hesitated to waste even more energy searching for something to burn, when all my other searches had been fruitless.

I pulled out the bundle, the smell wafting up into my nostrils, the burn rankling at my skin, and set it down in front of me. I unwrapped it, unfolding the intricately wrapped steak, the alien butcher tucking paper into folds, keeping the meat packed tight, and I opened the gift as a child on Christmas.

The smell filled the hallway I sat in, kneeling on the wooden boards, my pack next to me. I kneeled in a chemical mausoleum and tugged apart the bundle, revealing the dark meat. The twin desires filled me again, of revulsion and ecstasy, of desire and disgust. It pushed and pulled, and I couldn't imagine holding the god-steak in my mouth, its black blood filling my gums, covering my tongue, but I desperately needed it, my mouth watering. My stomach ached, sadly grumbling, days since I'd eaten anything.

I pulled my pocket knife from my belt and pressed it to the tip of the cut, and it slid neatly through, slicing the thinnest piece of meat from the edge.

I took a deep breath, licking my lips, and lifted it, the blood dripping onto the wooden floor of the maze, staining it. I opened my mouth and laid it on my tongue.

Yours Forever

It melted in my mouth, supremely tender, the softest cut, the truest gift, and I tasted the dastardly chemicals, my brain screaming at the wrongness of it, but I swallowed it down, wanting all of it, needing the god in me.

I sliced another piece, thicker now, craving more, despite the terror and disgust that bisected me, and I shoved it into my mouth, the meat falling apart before I could chew, filled with ammonia and bliss, sliding down my throat. Everything in me told me to stop, my body wanting the meat, and I continued, cutting slice after slice, and then using my hands, taking ragged chunks of the steak in my mouth, my hands and tongue stained black from the god's remnant blood.

I did not want to eat it, but I devoured the meat, my teeth dark, my mouth replete with the taste of death, and it filled me, my sad stomach engorged with god.

I was no longer hungry.

32

Without it, I would have died. I would have not lasted to find this salvation.

That is what I tell myself.

The godflesh sustained me for days. I explored further, knowing I would still need rations beyond it. The meat had created new processes in me, my body churning through the fuel it had given me, and I was energized again, moving through the endless maze.

I will not detail the tedium, of opening a hundred doors, of steadfastly marking my progress on the walls with chalk, of avoiding the shifting movement of the maze, and noting where and how it shifted, if I were to ever return.

But through that tedium, I realized how Morgan had become accustomed to this place. That after many days or weeks inside, you saw the patterns, the lefts and rights, the short and long hallways, the different rhythms as the maze shifted.

But after many a tiring hour, of scouting door after door, I found a salvation. I found an oasis.

I found a garden.

A garden of sorts, not of Eve and Adam, of plentiful fruit and vegetables, of animals that lay down before you and sacrifice their tender flesh, where trees and herbs grow bountiful, but it is a garden still, and surely must be where Suffolk and Morgan have supped countless times, to keep themselves stable in difficult hours down in the maze in search of you.

The garden was not grown by man, but by the nature of this world, wherever this door has taken me. It took all my willpower not to yelp with glee when I entered this place, the door closing behind me, but still there, still unlocked, a place to resupply whenever I was in need.

The mushrooms filled my vision. They were everywhere around me, of all sizes, of all colors, shapes defying my knowledge of fungi. I had studied them, as I had studied all things of the natural order, and my knowledge contained the strange shapes of common mushrooms of my Earth. They grew on trees, in caverns and barns, of the typical umbrella-shaped fruiting body, and then of the willowy discus, of the colors, of the delicious pulp and the dangerous poisons of them all.

These fungi defied all of my knowledge. Some soared above me, forty, fifty feet or higher, their stalks thick and woody, holding the tall towers aloft. Others were small, closer to my expectation, near my feet. But undisturbed, they would grow to mammoth size. I looked through the forest of mushrooms and saw only more.

I was in a rainforest, but the deciduous were only fungus, as far as the eye could see. It was plentiful, and I counted mushrooms as one of my favorite foods, when I could find them as sundries. They would serve as ample rations, and would keep well for many days, packed and stored properly. I had the proper knowledge, from my days foraging as a youth on my aunt's property.

But the fungi held another boon, one even more fateful, and that is one of the species, the color of a robin's egg, was bowl-shaped, growing into its own serving plate, and cradled in each of these mammoth fungi was an incredible pool of liquid. I say liquid, because I do not think it water, not in our typical sense.

I was tentative, unsure if this water would poison me. I smelled it, and it smelled pleasant, slightly sweet.

My water supply had never run out, not even in my most desperate hour, but it was in short threaten, and I would need more, just as I needed food. I dipped my hand, and it was cool, but not cold, and soothed my skin, still stained black. I cupped and held a small amount of the liquid, and took it to my mouth, and measured a sip between my lips.

I held it inside, and it was clean, and tasted neutral, and I waited a moment more, and then swallowed. It slid down my throat and soothed me, settling into my stomach.

I would wait, wait to see if there were any deleterious effects, while I examined the surrounding mushrooms. I had similar concerns about the toxicity of these fungi. In my youth, my aunt had warned against the "death caps", the brown, green, and white mushrooms, that grew everywhere in her woods, alongside their safe to eat cousins. But I also knew poisonous fungi were few and far between, with most breeds being safe to consume.

I glanced around, looking not up at the mushrooms that towered above me, but the ones that grew close to the ground, at my height or lower. Was there wildlife here? I hesitated to meet it, worried it might be dangerous, but I was concerned with anything that might consume the mushrooms as well. Anything that has been eaten must be safe for me, and I looked closely at the mushroom clusters, looking for sign of predation.

After searching, I spotted a cluster that had been picked through, clearly, repeatedly. Had it been a local animal? Or perhaps Morgan or Suffolk?

It did not matter, but I took it as a sign it was safe. I picked these, and soon found evidence of the same on several other variety, and picked those as well.

I will not bore you, Beloved, with my tales of harvesting mushrooms, but know I bundled and stacked them as my new rations, testing each for poisonous effects, and finding no ill will to my fortitude. Neither the water had I suffered, and I filled my tank with it. I bundled as much of the fungi I could carry and returned to the maze as I had entered. I took careful note of the location of the garden, if and when I would need to return.

The compass had thrummed, long ago, and I made my slow way back, my pack heavy with supplies.

33

I fear the godflesh is changing me.

I feel wrong, things subtly shifting, moving and growing inside me. I had worried the meal would hurt me, cause me impossible pain, a pain of wrongness inside, tearing me apart.

But a worse worry has replaced it.

The change is causing no pain at all.

I have continued on my journey with my rations restocked, following the vibration of the compass, thrumming in my chest, my skin humming as it hones in on the next door I should enter.

The thirteenth void is dark, and therefore not safe to return. But now stocked with rations, I was prepared.

The door swung shut behind me, locked, and I found myself in a house, a large home, but of old construction, made of stone and wood. Older than the home in Plainmoor certainly, the work of the elder Architect. How old it is, is impossible to tell. The wooden doors appear newer than the stonework that surrounds me, but the stone itself could be centuries old. Electric lanterns were strung up along the walls as I explored, as I must not only ponder the question of where, but of when.

Cycles, said Suffolk. The thought has not left me.

I explored, moving through what I thought was a home, exploring room by room. It was settled, but appeared empty. Drafty, but clean, with a slight smell of must and age. Not abandoned, but the residents seemed to have gone missing.

Or at least I hoped they had. After my previous encounters, I do not require another meeting with a resident of the maze's rooms. As I explored, my top priority was the second door. The sooner I could leave this place behind, the better.

Because despite my first inclination, this was not a house. It was a castle.

I explored hallways, looking for the door back to the maze, but found only more rooms, set up as bedrooms, as dens, as dining rooms. I found myself at a window, and looked out to see a foggy landscape, of craggy peaks and cliffs, the castle overlooking them, fog lifting high in the air, the ground disappearing somewhere underneath.

The environs were beautiful, but I sensed danger here, and my instincts told me to escape, to run, to find a way out. But that second door was my only hope, and I continued to search. I was on the top level of the castle, and after an exhaustive search, a door through, back to the maze, was not here.

And soon—soon I found the cause of my worry. As I walked down a staircase to a lower level, I heard a moaning. Not of pleasure, but of pain. Of a deep, unrelenting pain, that consumed a body and soul. I drew my pistol and kept my head up, looking for any attacker. I still only heard the groaning, and nothing else, and cautiously approached it, past hallways and doors, but never the second door. If I spied the second door, I would escape without a thought. I had reached the limit of what sating my curiosity was worth.

But without it, I went to the pain, and found it. It was an atrocity.

The creature was strapped to a table, with thick iron manacles, wrapped around wrists, ankles, and neck. It struggled weakly against them, but they were hard metal, attached to the table with heavy chain, too strong for anyone to break.

I say creature, because I do not know how else to describe the thing. As I witnessed it, I would say it was once human, once something approaching a person. But no longer.

It had mutated, into something unspeakable. I describe wrists and ankles, but those are vestigial words I use to describe what have become the awkward limbs of the creature. Its legs were long, longer than any human's legs, stretching out of proportion to the rest of it, seven feet long, thin, pulled like a taffy I would see at the fair as a child. Its arms were of normal length, but the fists were massive, bloated balls of bone and muscle, spikes of cartilage broken through the skin, softly leaking blood.

The torso was bulbous, with protruding pieces of what looked like coral life, inflating and deflating with the creature's breath.

And its face. Its face was inhuman, a writhing mass of tentacles, pink and pulsing, no eyes, no nose, only a primitive hole that was once a mouth, emitting a terrible moaning pain as it struggled at its bonds.

What had happened to this thing, this creature that perhaps once had been man?

I do not know, but I did not free it, or even attempt it. The only solace I could provide it was a bullet, but I hesitated to fire a gun in this place. The room was set up as a laboratory of sorts, with medical instruments within reach, but nothing I recognized, despite my time in the lab. They were not done with this poor wretch, and I left the room, ignoring its moans, searching for the second door. It was then I heard a door creaking open, from beyond the creature's home, and I retreated to an empty room, closing the door inside. I would send this missive before I continue further.

I have my pistol ready.

Wait, I hear them coming.

34

Beloved, help me, please.

The Scientist, he has captured me. I have been confined, stuck in a cell, waiting for my treatment. For whatever he has planned for me. He examined me, probed me, with the force of those brutes he controls, or has enslaved, or created.

They interrupted my last missive, and somehow knew my location, and they came in waves, the stout morlocks seeking me out in the grounds of the castle. I had my pistol ready, and I fired as they approached, hitting several, but only one went down, the others continuing, even with chunks blown through them, and they seized me, taking my gun, and my things, and dragging me through the castle, and down, down, down into the lower levels, into the lab.

It is a laboratory of sorts, they pulled me down into, and they stripped me, pulling my clothes off, leaving me naked, and then strapping me down with thick leather straps, and then abandoning me to the cold air, my head immobile. No matter how I struggled, the straps would not relent, and then after an interminable length of time, the Scientist himself appeared, large in my vision as he approached.

He was a massive man, over six and a half feet tall, broad of shoulder, thick at the hip. His arms and legs bulged, but unnaturally. I quickly surmised he did not come by his size innately, as I saw the dense scarring at his arms and legs, having done something to himself to create the mass.

His face was similarly distorted, his head larger than natural, and I saw more scars. His smile was big, his skin smooth, his hair perfectly coiffed. He had the look of a doll, despite his eyes being the only remaining part of him that was still him, unable to be perverted like the rest of his body. At least not yet.

The Scientist did not move smoothly, his arms and legs always in a loping motion, never in a straight line, surely a product of his deformed gait and size, and he poked and prodded at me.

"What do you want with me?" I asked him.

"Hush hush hush," he whispered to me, as he peered into my open eyes, and pushed apart my teeth. I bared down on them, grinding them together, nearly catching his fingers, and he called for a brute, and two came in, and stuck their dirty fingers into my mouth, and pried my jaw open, and the Scientist looked inside again, and he gasped, and then smiled.

"You have tasted the Anargh!" he exclaimed. "I can smell it on your breath, in your skin. Excellent, excellent news. Such a ripe fruit you are." He motioned to the brutes, and they let go of my mouth, and I spit their dirty leavings out. Some of the spittle hit the Scientist, but he made no motion to clean himself. He moved onto my armpits, and my torso, and my nethers, sticking his fingers inside me, and I gritted my teeth.

He returned to my torso, and rubbed his hands over my bare stomach, and poked, pressing deeply. He touched me, more than an examination, but instead, a caress, a loving touch, as he felt the presence inside.

"I can feel it," he said, and returned to standing, smiling at me. "Young man, you are a ripe fruit indeed. You are special, even. This will take some time."

And then he left, and the brutes returned, and unbound me, but gave me no clothes, nothing, and put me in this cell, my only company the wasting corpses of previous victims.

I tried to take in my surroundings, but there was little to go on. This castle is lit with electric light, and it looks out on Earthly climes, but surely this cannot be my Earth. There is nothing on Earth above that resembles this Scientist.

He speaks of the godflesh, and its having taken root in me. I worry, worry about his intentions.

The look on his face—he intends something ominous. Something that makes me think the moaning victim in the castle above would be a mercy if I had the choice. I have no clothes, no supplies, my gun lost above.

I beg you, Beloved. Please, if you truly are listening. If you are there—help me. Send me aid, a blessed sword with which I can smite these deviants, or a key to this dastardly cell.

Anything, anything.

I beg you.

35

Please, Beloved. Please.

I do not know how long it has been. I cannot see the sun. I have been fed, and watered, given a bowl of each every day. I assume it is every day, but I do not know. The food is a thick gruel, a gray sludge I resisted eating, but my aching stomach urged me to force it down.

It has sustained me. The Scientist does not wish me to die, not from malnutrition or starvation.

I must live, so that he may test.

That is what I have become, Beloved.

I have been kept in my cell for days, a brute returning to feed me periodically. I have made waste in the corner, and have done my best to cover it, but the cell stinks. They have yet to give me clothes, and I have taken fitful sleep curled in the furthest spot from my toilet.

It has been misery. This decrepit space is heaven compared to the lab where I have been taken. It is not the same room as where I was previously examined.

It is a larger space, filled with tables and arcane equipment, paraphernalia unrecognizable to my trained eye. These tools were not made on Earth, not my Earth, wherever I may be. Or perhaps the Scientist fashioned them himself, necessary for his deranged experiments. They are horrific, metal instruments, jagged, prying, meant to tuck and pull at tissues without regard for pain or trauma.

The brutes grabbed me from my cell and carried me there. I fought, but was too weak to stop them, as they strapped me to a table in the larger lab, my body exposed under an array of electric light shining into my eyes. I closed them, to avoid a terrible blindness, but opened them again when the Scientist returned, the brutes all standing at the ready, out of my sight. All parts of me were strapped down, and I was helpless, truly helpless.

"What are you doing, please?" I asked, but he ignored me, caressing my torso, as he had on our first meeting, then pushing hard, and I felt a resistance inside, something that should have felt foreign, not native, the godflesh I consumed building something inside of me.

"There we are," he said, his massive face filled with teeth, grinning at the thought of what was inside me.

"What are you doing to me?" I asked again, and he paused, and then finally considered me, his massive skull approaching my eyes, his breath hot in my face. The skin on his head was stretched taut, strained to its ripping point, and his original eyes stared at me.

"I'm going to help you grow, young man," he said. "You are the most promising yet. We will find home in you."

"What—what does that—"

"Hush hush hush," he said, and he gestured to the brutes, who came and forced open my mouth, shoving a gag between my teeth and tying it tight, and I could not talk, only managing grunts and noises as I tried. "I will need silence as I operate. Concentration is paramount. We cannot have a spoilage."

My heart thudded in my chest, and the table was wet beneath me as I sweat, darkness filling me. If I had only known his plans—I would have resisted the brutes more.

The Scientist grabbed a black pen of sorts from his tray, and wrote on my torso, tracing the path of the godflesh inside me. He traced lines and circles, and then the pen was put down.

I tried to yell, tried to ask why, why, but the gag stopped it all, and then he revealed a blade, not a scalpel, but larger, something his massive paws could handle, but just as sharp, and it glinted underneath the lights, and I closed my eyes and held my breath, forcing my mind away, anywhere but here.

I felt pressure on my torso at first, just pressure, but then searing pain followed, and I had to see, I couldn't look but I had to know, had to see the operation, and I opened my eyes, and craned my head as much as I could.

I should not have looked.

One should not look and see the fragile state of one's own flesh. The Scientist carved through my skin, the blade easily slicing through the top layer, through the muscle, and I screamed, the pain hitting me in full now. I screamed and screamed into my gag, but the Scientist did not stop, continuing to cut until a massive hole was open in my torso, and he peeled back the skin and muscle, revealing my bowels.

"Ah, yes," he said, speaking between his teeth, caressing a stone black organ next to my intestines, my intestines, my Beloved, please, please help me.

He touched it, feeling it, as he had through my skin.

I screamed still, sweat pouring down my face.

"Hush hush," he said. "The pain is rudimentary, young man. It will not kill you. And any painkiller might spoil the blessing. Do not worry, it will not take long. A simple thing, but blessed."

I struggled against my bindings, but they did not relent, and I watched him put down his blade, and retrieved something else, something unrecognizable as medical instrument.

"The implant," he said, smiling at me. "It will help you grow." It was a thin stone, a soft pink, iridescent underneath the lights. He grabbed a rag and polished it a final time and then moved it toward me.

I shouted, yelled no with all my might, but it meant nothing, and he slid the pink stone inside me, and I felt a strange attraction from within, some horrible rhythm as the pink implant slid alongside the godflesh organ, the two locking into place, and I felt a sudden churning, an immediate rush of movement, between my organs, and then an even larger outburst of pain, and I screamed, biting down hard on my gag, and then I saw only blackness.

I awoke as he sewed me up, stitching the enormous rent in my flesh closed, his large fingers pulling me back together. My blood still pounded, and tears flowed down my cheeks, but the pain had relented, an incredible ache smaller than the fountain of torment that had ripped through my body just moments ago.

He finished sewing, and I looked, and I was one piece again, black thread marking my body like a map, where the Scientist had lain his claim.

"All done for today," he said, happy with himself, his voice ebullient. "You did well, young man. We will examine the results in a week's time." He left, gone, departed, and then the brutes manhandled me again, taking me from the lab back to my cell. I did not struggle, my strength all but gone, worried too much movement would rupture the terrible wound in me.

It has been days since the surgery, and I examine the wound, each day waking, and hoping it was a nightmare, something to be forgotten, wiped like a clean slate from my mind.

But the stitches remain, and I touch the wound, worrying it will be infected, worrying the strange work of the Scientist will kill me.

But there are no signs of infection. None at all. It defies my knowledge of medicine.

There are other signs.

Signs of growth.

My stomach bulges, and there is movement.

I do not know what is inside me.

Please, send me salvation, Beloved.

36

Salvation, salvation, my Beloved. It is to you I dedicate my effort, this quest I will not fail.

The brutes visited me again, a week after the operation, when the smooth pink stone was inserted inside me, wedded to a pitch black organ, grown from the godflesh I had consumed.

My thoughts in that time were only to you, of waiting, hoping for help you would send me.

But I was a fool. I was sent here to rescue you, and you had already given me so much for me to make it to this point. The begging and pleading would not help me. I must help myself. I must save you.

I examined the surroundings of my cell once again. I looked at the corpses I shared it with. Two of them, both humanoid, but neither human. They had been naked as well, but their flesh had mostly rotted away, leaving behind a thin layer of tissue covering a skeleton.

They were beyond rot, their age untellable from a brief examination. And I had thought myself without a tool in this cell, unable to pick the lock, incapable of escape.

And I was right, at least in that regard. But I had given up on salvaging something from their bodies too easily. I waited until the brutes were out of hearing range, and pulled at the skin of one corpse, pulling away the dried flesh that surrounded its hand. I needed the bones within, and soon I found them, and ripped off any remaining flesh.

The bones were dry underneath, and I looked at them one by one, until I found the perfect specific, a small bone in the wrist that would serve my purposes. I wrenched it loose with a pop, and then rubbed the edge against the stone wall. Over and over, over and over, and soon the stone ground away at the bone, leaving a sharpened end, but it needed to be sharper still, and minute enough for me to palm. After only an hour of work, it was suitable. I briefly tested its strength, and it was strong enough. Enough was all I needed.

The brutes came back, a week after my implant, and pulled me to my feet and back to the lab. I did not struggle, not even slightly, holding onto the strength I had.

I had consumed every ounce of the sludge they fed me, and had exerted myself as little as possible in the intervening days. I would need the constitution when the time came.

And it was approaching.

They carried me to the same lab, and strapped me down, all the same.

But as they tied me down, I waited, holding, concentrating. I held the bone in my left hand, and as they pushed down my left wrist underneath the leather bindings, I flexed my arm as much as I could, without drawing the attention of the brute.

They finished, and retreated, and I softly tested the limits of my bounds. I pulled slightly at my left wrist, and the bindings were loose. If I pulled hard, I could slide it through, perhaps losing only a small bit of skin in the bargain.

I waited.

The Scientist came along quickly, wearing similar clothes as before, loose black clothing sewn to fit his bulky frame.

He smiled at me again, looking into my eyes before staring at my torso. His hands pressed against it, and something moved inside as a result, in response. I held my breath.

"Let us check on your growth," he said, smiling. "You are perhaps under ripe, but we will see. We will snip you open, and see what fruits."

He turned to grab his blade, to cut me back open, but no, today, I would be my savior, to be thine.

I pulled hard on my left wrist, yanking free of the leather strap, scraping at my skin as I slid it out. I let the sharp piece of bone loose from inside my fist and reached out and stabbed the Scientist in the eye, aiming for the perfect brown eye that had never been altered or changed. It sunk deep inside and the Scientist yelled out in pain, and flailed at me, but he couldn't see, and I reached, reached, and grabbed his blade, and pulled it to my other hand, slicing through the leather quickly. I cut through the binding on my neck and sat up, forcing myself up with all my strength. Two brutes charged in to help, and I swung at them with the blade, slicing one's throat, and stabbing the other in the torso, the Scientist's massive scalpel an ample killing tool. A third came in and I sliced across its face, and it screamed in pain, a high-pitched squeal, and ran.

The Scientist staggered back, pulling the bone stiletto from his eye, and I sliced through the straps at my ankles, and stood up, facing him. He considered me with his only eye, his vast mouth turned in a grimace.

"Oh, you will pay for that, young man," he said, and he charged me with all his size. But he only had a single eye, and I stepped to his left, to his blind side, and he missed me, crashing into the lab table and knocking over his tray of equipment. I didn't wait, and jumped onto his back, latching onto his neck with one arm, and stabbing him in the head repeatedly with his own scalpel. It sunk into his skin, over and over, and he got up, trying to throw me off, but I held on, stabbing him in the neck, the blade hitting his windpipe, and I squeezed the handle in my fist, and dug, moving the blade back and forth.

He struggled, and then fell to his knees, gargling, blood pouring from his wounds, onto the ground. My hands were coated in it, but I held on tight as he collapsed, heaving a heavy last breath before dying.

I climbed off him, pulling the blade with me, covered in his blood. I panted, all of my energy used smiting this terrible man. The third brute, who I had slashed, cowered along the back corner of the lab. I approached it, covered in its master's blood.

"Where are my things?" I asked. "Take me." It scrambled, bleeding from the gash on its face, and it led me to a room, a small pantry filled not just with my things, my supplies and gun, but many other packs. The Scientist had done this to many. He had taken advantage of the route to your heart coming through his castle, and he had picked the fruit that hung low in his face.

I grabbed my belongings, and looked through the rest, salvaging what I could, stuffing useful things into my bag. I could inventory them later. The brute waited quietly nearby, its face downcast.

"Where is the second door?" I asked, turning to it. I waited, to see if it understood, but it didn't hesitate, and led me further, down another set of stairs, and down another, and through twisting hallways, passing past bedrooms, past dining rooms, past what the castle had once been before it became the demented arboretum of the mad Scientist.

I saw the door then, as we turned a corner. I still carried the Scientist's blade in my hand, and I kept it. It had proven itself. I considered the brute only for a moment, now masterless, bleeding, but then I moved on, opening the door, and walking through.

I will soon save you, Beloved.

37

I am close to you.

I have escaped the Scientist and have returned to the maze. I did not stop after my last missive, continuing onward and through. The compass has thrummed stronger now as I approach the path to you, harder than it has before, and it vibrates in my heart.

I take it as a sign. I must be near your heart, near the end of this accursed journey, almost having solved the maze.

I have gone through several doors, pushing through them, with none near horror of several I have passed through. There were no brutes to capture me, no desertous treks.

Each was a window into a new world, some version of my Earth I would not reside in, or other realms, inhospitable to humanity for anything longer than a short while.

I passed through them, walking through a door, and finding its second.

I noted them in my notebook, the coordinates, now having seen thousands of doors.

I noted the world of steel, a smooth world of metal and brass.

I noted the insects, the mass rolling across the void.

I noted the angels who sang to me from the parallel, sirens who called for my heart, a test of my faith in you. They failed to sway me. They underestimated my strength and conviction.

My hand went to my stomach, feeling the rolling ball of movement every so often, the black organ pressing against my insides, the pink implant spurring ever onward its growth. It had grown before, I knew it had, but the Scientist's work had sped its evolution. The stitches were healing still, and within days I could cut them out.

But there was a part of me that wanted to rip at my seams, to pull the pink implant and that dark organ from my bowels, and then seal myself back up, and toss those alien pieces from the bridge I tread, down into the chasm, down into the abyss.

But I couldn't. I felt the mother to them. I would sooner rip the womb from you.

I noted the worlds as I passed through them.

The compass hums now, practically singing as I speak to you.

I noted the bridge.

The bridge did test me, as I have a failing of heights. I stood so high, and it spanned a distance incalculable. A fall from a height that would surely kill. I would reach terminal velocity and then continue, breaking my body on impact.

But as I forced myself across the bridge, the compass singing in my chest, I worried there was only a fall. I told myself not to look down, into the void, but I did, and I was right, there was no bottom, there was only the fall, and the fall would kill me, slowly, an eternal gravity that would hold me until I starved.

But I crossed it to the second door. I traveled, my food supplies running low again, but there was the mushroom garden, and I could retrace my steps, but the vibration was constant, louder and louder as I left the bridge, and entered the maze once again, now shaking me so hard I could not sleep, so close to you.

I attempted sleep, but it was impossible, my body shaking from the metal trembling, and I gave up, using my rations as a substitute for rest, eating the slabs of mushroom I had carved from the garden. My eyes ached, begging for sleep, but the compass shook, shook.

You are near.

I continued, pushing through another set of doors, doing my best to listen to the shaking song of the guiding instrument.

Every door I hoped was a simple world, an easy path between doors, but they were not easy, no room was easy, I have realized that. All come with a price. Some are merely simpler to pay.

I noted the worlds as I passed through.

I paid their price and paid it gladly. You lay on the other side.

I have stopped for a rest. A rest it can only be, for the compass vibrates so hard my teeth shake, and my blood trembles. I had questioned myself, picking up the device, pulling it from the corpse of the elder Suffolk, of the dead Architect, but now it has become invaluable. I would have never located you without it, would never have been able to traverse the many doors without its help.

The Architect would have found you, I've realized. If it was not for the Hounds, he would have succeeded, leaving me a failure.

But the Hounds did hunt him.

How long had they hunted?

I picture it, in my mind's eye. A story.

Suffolk, the younger, exploring the maze, searching for you, entering through an obelisk. In a moment of weakness, of lack of focus, Suffolk perceives the Hounds.

He runs, runs for his life. Leaves the maze, and thinking he has escaped the Hounds, starts a life.

Falls in love. Starts a family.

But the Hounds pursue tirelessly, even across the bounds of space and time.

They find him.

They find his wife and child.

They perceive as well, and they are not fit for the chase.

Suffolk escapes. Builds the House, and re-homes the maze. Brings it to a more controlled place.

He delves once more. Perhaps to rid himself of the Hounds. To use your heart for such a purpose.

I do not know. It is only a story.

The compass thrums, and your heart is through one more door. I know it. We will escape, Beloved.

38

I have never come closer to you.

I was right, I was on the precipice. The verge of rescuing you, on the edge of caressing you for the first and final time and pulling you from this maze, and reuniting you. Extracting your kidnapped heart, and returning it to the world.

I noted the constellation on the door, the coordinates, another seven lights, making note of the light and the void and it was a door without a simple return, but I had no intention of returning. If the second door led to your heart, I would blast straight through hell and inferno to find you.

The door opened and closed behind me, but I did not look backward. I examined the path before me.

It was a simple room.

A room I had been in before.

It was the simple square room, one of the first I had visited in the maze, long before I had grasped the completeness of what this place was. It had been a simple room, the exit door on the other side.

The exit was still there, and I nearly rushed to it, to get through the other side, to get closer to you. But I paused.

For I remembered what had been in the room.

A stack of bodies. Corpses. Long dead, dessicated. Stacked alongside the right wall as I entered.

But they were not here now.

I checked the coordinates, flipping back in my notebook, hundreds of pages backward, and sure enough, it was the same coordinates. The same room.

I had found myself in the same room, so much deeper in the maze. But no bodies.

Had someone taken them?

I did not know, but your heart lay through the other side, and I did not waste time pondering uncertainties and unnecessaries. I noted the lack of bodies in my notebook and went through the second door.

I saw you, then.

You were close, closer than before, in the early delving days, when I saw a peek of you before the maze had cut you off. The compass sung so loudly, it screamed, a second heart.

But it was not the only thing that shook. The floor shuddered as well, already quaking as I exited the door, and I saw it. The maze was preparing to shift again, to pull me away from you, to separate us. I would not, could not. Not again, not with you so close.

Your heart was there, floating there, on the altar, pure white stone, your holy organ meant for it and it for you, holding in the space, put there by the jealous, by the dark, by the evil men who would keep you from the world, and hide you here away from our salvation.

Less than a hundred feet, and my fingers trembled at the thought of an embrace, and I waited no longer, sprinting toward you. The ground shook, the wooden boards preparing to move again, to silo you away, to lead me astray once more, but I would not, not another trek, not another hundred doors, where I would be tested and tortured and strung through a thousand guerrilla worlds.

I sprinted, my feet pounding on the wooden boards, and you were close, closer, and I saw every detail of you, and I would hold you, and carry you out of here like a newborn babe, and present you to the Earth, where you would ascend to your rightful place, and I would be the first to bow.

The maze threatened to shift, but I would beat it this time. I would succeed, where all others had failed. You were almost within reach, the maze not yet shifted, and triumph soared in my heart, I would succeed.

A single corridor away, and I was taken off my feet, the breath driven from me.

I shook my head, dazed, forcing my way up, but it held me down, and I tilted my head up, only to see your heart shift away from me. The maze tilted, either it or me, and then your heart was gone, the hallway gone, only wall remaining, a dead end. The compass in my heart died then, the screaming song vanishing in an instant.

Tears formed at the corners of my eyes, but then transformed into rage, and I reached for my pistol. I would kill whatever had stopped me, whatever latest obstacle that had once again stolen you from me.

But my revolver was gone, no longer in the holster.

"I don't think so, pup," said Morgan, holding it. He stood to the side of me, having tackled me, disarmed me, and climbed away. He pointed it at me, freezing me, my anger impotent. "You cannot have her. Not that easy." And his smile appeared, wavered, and stayed.

And then he ran back down the way I had come, and then turning, and out of sight.

I shouted and jumped to my feet, and sprinted after him. He had the pistol, but I did not care, I would catch him, and punish him. I should have killed him, I should have killed him, but I would do it now, regardless of his physical superiority or his stolen gun. You fueled me, and I would chase him and kill him with your righteousness.

I turned down the hallway after him and watched him jump through a doorway, and I ran after and went through afterward.

I emerged in a tunnel, the door in the sidewall. Train tracks lay before me. A subway tunnel? It looked nothing like the tunnels I had seen, the tracks heavy and thick, but I did not have time.

I saw in the dim light a shadow sprint down the shaft, and I sprinted after him, after the Lover, the Fiend.

I ran hard, my chest heaving, my heart bursting with pain, with rage, with sorrow, I will find him, I will kill him.

I ran through the darkness, and then a light approached. The ground shook, cacophony filling the air. A train rushed toward me, and I saw it, and I dove into a side passage, a small alcove to shelter myself.

The train thundered past.

It thunders past still, hours later.

39

The train passed after some time. I swore at it, spitting defiant words at the cramped alcove I was trapped in. Furious rage had captured me, and would not let go, despite the time of the passing train.

The train was not of my time, or my place, and it was dark inside. I did not venture to investigate. It was only an obstacle. I had no time for mysteries and puzzles of infinite doors and worlds. I needed the Lover. I needed to show him the fury of his betrayal, of his intervention, of his aiding the capture of you!

How dare he, the monster, the rogue, the traitor!

When I saw the end of the train approaching, I gathered my things, and hurried, running after the exit door. I followed the tunnel, and there, just around the bend was the second door. Had Morgan known the timing of the train, and used it to escape me? I would not put it past him, the scoundrel. He had been here a countless eon, cagey about his past, and his reasons, and he knew the doors better than I. He owned some intrinsic knowledge, something gained from being here, in proximity to the maze, or you, or both. And that infuriated me more.

But I did not give up. I ran after him, hoping there was a trail, some sort of way to track him.

I entered back into the maze, through another door, and there was no sign of him. I paused, listening, but heard nothing, no sound, not the distant echo of his footsteps, or his harried breathing as he went to his next door.

No sound betrayed him, and I thought, searching my mind for any means to find him. There had to be a way, had to be. The compass was silent, had been silent ever since you had shifted away, and did not pulse no matter which direction I walked.

I considered the man and remembered.

His musk. The smell of sinew and sweat, and dirt, and grime.

I stopped myself again, and I smelled. My nose had never been a spectacular sense, but Morgan's scent was powerful, and I placed my nose to the ground, where his feet surely would have stepped. I would be the bloodhound and would find this Lover. I would bring him to your justice.

On hands and knees, I crawled, following the smell of his footsteps, my knees thudding on the wooden floorboards, following his dastardly odor.

It brought me to a door, and I rejoiced. I stood up and entered.

I was through before I realized I had not noted the starfield.

No matter the coordinates. The Lover was still on my mind, and I found myself in a thick jungle, and the door behind was gone.

The air was dense, heavy with water, and I had never been in jungle like this in my life, having seen thick forest, but nothing like this, not seen outside the deepest jungle of Africa or South America. There was just enough light to see, whatever sunlight here blocked by the tree canopy.

The canopy towered over me, and water fell on me, my shirt soon soaked through, in a mixture of sweat and humidity.

I had no desire to fight through this impenetrable fauna, but it had a positive. It confirmed The Lover had come this way, that I could trust my nose. And he had needed to cut through himself, and had done so, a clear path of destruction leading ahead and then to the right. Morgan was ahead, and I followed. My feet sunk into the soft mud, staining my shoes, and water seeped into my feet, but I continued, following his trail. It was a simple path to follow, the jungle overgrown in every other direction.

I listened and heard nothing but the fall of rain. Surely, there would be predators. I've heard of great cats and of terrible serpents stalking the distant jungles of the world, but I saw no evidence of them here.

I followed Morgan's trail, moving as fast as my feet would carry me through the rough terrain. How deep was this jungle? How far had Morgan traversed? How much time had been stolen from me by the train?

I followed, and then I came to the river. I had no other words for it, a massive pool of flowing dark water. The canopy broke, and I saw the sky, but it was dim, a dark sky, and I looked up, and I saw it then.

The coordinates. The thirteen voids, all lit here. They shone dully, not one as bright as my Sun, but in concordance they lit this jungle well enough.

The dark river flowed. Morgan's path led to it. I would have to ford it, or swim it. I doubted Morgan had a boat, and so I removed my pack, and put it over my head, and stepped into the water, testing the current. It tugged at me, but I still could stand, and I moved forward, testing each step. My pack was light, most of my mushroom rations gone, but still it carried many other supplies, and my arms ached as I forded the water.

I stepped, the water reaching my shins, then thighs, then hips, and then it was above my belly button. I fought with each step, the current strong, but I was almost halfway across, and had seen the worst of it. It would not grow any stronger, surely.

My arms trembled, holding the bag above my head, and then I took a step, and with only one foot down, the current caught me, and I tumbled, and then I was under, and I fought to hold on to my pack, and to keep my head above water, but the river forced the choice, and I chose air, letting my pack go, paddling my way back to the surface, and then swimming hard, hand over hand, arm over arm, and soon I could touch again, and I surfaced, only hip deep, and then stood, and walked to the shore, soaking wet, my pack gone, swept downstream.

"You look like a sad wet dog," said Morgan, and he was there, sitting on an overturned tree, my gun in his hand, resting in his lap. He stared at me in the dim light.

"You son of a bitch—" I started, and he raised the pistol as I made to charge. He did not smile.

"No," he said. "Not here."

"You stopped me," I said. "I was on the verge of greatness."

"You're not ready."

"Who are you to judge?" I asked. "You are a mere man, a rogue, a scoundrel. You are not fit to measure if I can handle her heart, you know nothing—"

"You are so confident," he said. "I remember those days. The maze will humble you."

"Humble me?" I asked. "I have crawled through the misbegotten desert, have eaten godflesh, have felt the Scientist's implant grow in me—"

"No," he said, coldly. "No. You will see. And it is not my judgment. It is hers. She told me you were not ready. That you needed further growth."

"You arrogant whelp, how dare you—" I charged at him again, and he calmly stood and struck me across the face with my pistol, and a flare of pain sparked with a crack as my nose broke. I fell backwards, blood pouring down into my mouth.

"How dare you," he said, standing over me. "To think because you seized some contraption of a broken man that you could handle the heart of our Beautiful? A foolish pup, indeed."

"You know nothing," I said. "She is my Beloved. I will rescue her."

"Look at you," he said. "Look at you. Are you ready?"

I said nothing, my face broken. I stared up at him under the light of the Thirteen. "I—"

"Prove or be proven, pup," he said, and then threw my pistol into the river past me. "Follow me to the door. Prove yourself." And then he sprinted into the jungle, down a well-trod path.

I laid there, my skin soaked, blood pouring from my ruined nose. I picked myself up and pushed myself to my feet. I walked, my legs aching, dripping. I followed his path. I found the second door.

I am back in the maze. I have nothing except the ruined clothing of a dead man. There is no sign of the Lover.

Is it true, Beloved?

Am I not ready?

40

It has been some time since my last missive.

I have searched for the Lover. His wet footprints extended down multiple hallways, but then they dried up, and I was left with nothing, as numerous branching hallways extended off to the right and left and ahead and, after a turn, more intersecting hallways.

A hundred doors were there, in that scant stretch of maze, and he could have gone down any of them.

My notebook was gone, washed away in the dark river, never to be seen again, along with my notes about the doors I had visited, and the path that led to you.

I had no food, no water, no supplies at all. I had only the maze. Even the compass, which still lived in me, did not vibrate, or thrum, or sing. Since approaching you, it had been quiet. I hope yet still it will activate again. It led me to you. Maybe it will do it once more.

I searched, opening every door marked safe with a thirteenth void. I found some water in a small pond near the door, in a world of chirping frogs and massive lily pads, a stone bridge leading away from the entrance. I did not pursue the second door, not yet.

I drank my fill, even with the water dirty. If it would kill me, then I would die.

I stared at the coordinates after exiting. Six voids lit, seven empty. I stared, and my mind bent, a twinge, a fold, my senses curving.

This supply of water would hold me, but I could not trust it to be there if I traversed. I would need to find more, always find more, until I could find a canteen of some sort. Morgan did not carry one. Did he truly trust he could find water wherever the maze took him? That was madness. Every room was a trap.

But he had survived, somehow.

I explored further. Hunger pangs wracked my body. Time had passed, the damnable passage of untrackable time. I returned to the pond and found the source of the chirping frogs. I caught them, and I ate them. I retched, the creatures slimy in my mouth, their guts tasting like rotten eggs, but I swallowed them down by the handful, swallowing the pond water afterward, washing the taste from my mouth.

My stomach roiled at the raw meat, but it eventually stopped. My hunger had waned.

I explored further. I eventually exhausted all my options nearby, and traversed through the frog world, crossing the stone bridge, and went through the second door.

I explored further.

I stared at the coordinates of every door I opened, letting the Thirteen look back into me. My mind bent, and I did not resist. I did not take note of coordinates with paper and pen. The Thirteen spoke to me. I let them imprint themselves onto my mind.

As I explored, thoughts of Morgan didn't leave me. He lurked there, the vision of his smile, his wavering smile. He grinned at me there, his dark eyes boring into me, even in his absence. He had cost me you, and then dared to tell me I wasn't ready. Dared to say he spoke with your voice, the Blasphemer, the Traitor!

If I was not ready, how would I have made it to the maze? I bought the House, I found the stairwell, I discovered the maze, and crossed through a hundred worlds in pursuit of you. I did what was necessary, at every step, and Morgan, the madman, the Lover, who has yet to rescue you, dares to say I am not ready? And goes even further, and invokes your name, calls you Beautiful, and says his actions are driven by your words?

I have not forgotten him.

I explored further, and instead of my notebook, I collected coordinates in my mind. I mapped them all, seeing them, and letting them see me. Had I missed this? Was my notebook a trap?

I have not forgotten him. Prove myself, he said. Prove or be proven. I will find him, no matter how deep this maze moves, or how many worlds I cross. I know he is here, somewhere, within reach. Or just outside of it.

But it is clear I misunderstood him the entire time. He had never left my orbit, circling me perpetually. He had watched me from the edges, like a predator, stalking me, keeping his wavering smile always on the verge of discovery.

The maze was infinite, but the Lover was never interested in saving you. He is a predator, a danger. He is a captor, a jailer, just like the maze itself. Had he stolen you? Or has he become an accomplice to the prison?

It does not matter. Whatever he is, I will find him. I will never rescue you while he breathes.

I explore further.

41

It has been some time since my last missive.

How long, I do not know.

I have explored further, and the Thirteen have imprinted on me. I travel light, like Morgan. Despite his blasphemy, I have understood how he has survived down here for so long.

I have fashioned a knife. It is made from a dark stone, that I found in a cave world, long abandoned. I wrapped it with leather and thin cord, and now it stays with me.

I carry a canteen. Morgan does not, but I sacrifice the added weight for the surety of water.

Hunger pangs have become a friend. Food is much harder to come by, be it plant or animal, and I have stretched my appetite to its breaking point.

But I have crossed through many worlds, some fantastic, and some mundane.

I crossed them, and took stock of my surroundings, and imprinted the Thirteen, and moved through.

I have learned much, and now know what doors to avoid, the homes of mad Scientists, or treacherous desert crossings. I avoid the path of the Architect, and therefore the Hounds.

There is always a way through, but it may not be the obvious path.

I occasionally will pause in the hallways, and hear a distant footstep. The echo of a breath, or catch the musky smell of the Lover in the air. He is nearby. I know he is. I will find him.

But I am hardening. When I find him, I will be ready.

Only one thing gives me pause.

The unholy growth of the thing inside me.

The godflesh has grown, continues to grow, as time passes. I asked for a watch, aside from my hunger, and I was given one, with the consumption of deity, and the pink slate serving as incubator, given to me by the malformed Scientist, before I bled him onto the stone floor of his castle laboratory.

It has shifted, the abnormal organ kicking in the womb, as it's grown. It has been siphoning nutrients from me, surely, a child of god growing within. The bulge is unsightly now, no way to deny or ignore it, as it has grown. The skin of my lower left abdomen has stretched and stretched, and there are days I worry I will burst at the seams, but the skin remains whole.

But I know the growth still lives and grows and breathes. It is alive inside me, and with the addition of the implanted stone, it expands fast, faster. It swells beneath my skin, and sometimes, I feel the urge to take my obsidian blade and cut it out from inside me, to be my own surgeon, and remove the godly growth, and excise it from my body, and finally become whole again.

A goodly amount of fear remains, though. I do not have any surgical tools, nor bandage, nor replacement blood, nor stitches. I could remove the godtumor, but I may bleed out onto the wooden floor, and be found by the next delver.

Yes, I know there are more. A stream of them. The Lover, myself, Suffolk—we are but a sampling of the men who have come down into the depths in search of you. I have seen them come and go in my exploring, as I have dived into a deeper understanding of the hallways. I have let them be.

They will learn.

And I leave the growing organ be, as well. It remains inside, kicking, bulbous, but has not disrupted me, not yet.

I fear the day where it forces a birth, however. My stone knife is at the ready.

Will my child be friendly?

Or will it consume me from within?

The Lover remains at the forefront. Soon, I will encounter him again. As time has vanished from me, he still is there. He cost me everything.

Soon, I will make him pay.

42

A great deal of time has passed, Beloved. My deepest apologies. But I would not devote the time to a message when there was work to be done. When I was but a work in progress, still delving, still learning.

I have studied the Thirteen in this time. I once watched Morgan glance at a door and enter without hesitation. I boggled at the audacity to test what lay behind a door without pause or thought.

But I understand now, understand the language of the Thirteen. The language of the doors, of a constellation well beyond ours, the language of traversing worlds and testing limits.

I have honed myself down to my sharpest point. It was a necessary step, and if Morgan meant for me to prepare myself, I did not take his critique lightly. I am made of iron now, hardened by the maze, even with the god organ pulsing inside me, kicking its deific feet.

It no longer grows, itself satisfied in me, but I know it is only a matter of time before it tires of my skin. It wants the open air.

But a great deal of time has passed, and I have made progress. I found Morgan.

His smell, his musk, it gave him away, once again. The scent was ingrained in me, residing in my nostrils, and whenever I caught the aroma of him, I waited, paused, and pursued it to its natural end. I came up empty many times, but my justice for him was patient.

I stalked him on his trail, and I followed it, my nose to the ground, watching for any other sign of him. He had stayed in my orbit, I know he had, and there were moments where I felt his eyes on me, from down a long hallway, or from a vantage point in a world I did not know.

But Morgan was not a god. He was just a man, fallible, weak, and he would falter.

I stalked him and found him. He was resting, sitting near a fire in a world of dark. It was a place of sand, flat, but not a desert, not that I could see. I followed his scent to the door, and it opened into the murky realm of sand, no lights, no stars, no sun, just a dark sky, and shadowy landscape, lit only by Morgan's fire, hundreds of feet away, a glimpse of light on the horizon.

I crept slowly toward the light, the dark plain surrounding me. The sand slightly crunched below my feet, my shoes long replaced by moccasins of my creation, cut from the leather of a burrowing creature I killed in the tunnels of a forgotten world. The sandy plain was quiet, and I slowed, moving as stealthily. I saw him then, crouched next to the fire. He stared into it, the Lover, I had found him, after such long delving, a quest within reach, much like your heart had been taken from me.

He had robbed me of you, robbed you of freedom, and I would end this, here and now.

I approached, and he grew, and he crouched near the fire, and I came from behind, the only sound from me the scuffling of the sand. I gripped my stone blade, the edge razor sharp. It had been whetted with the blood of the meteor crabs of the asteroid ocean and had carved through the curtains of flesh within the bloated whale. I kept it sharp, a dangerous weapon.

The crackling fire filled my ears as I came close, the massive shadow of Morgan's form filling my eyes. I would end this, finally.

"If you mean to end me, pup, best do it quick," he said, and I leaped on him from behind, and sunk the knife into him. He moved at the last moment and the strike meant for his heart instead sunk into his shoulder, in between his neck and arm, and he shouted in pain, and I tried to pull out the blade, but it had become lodged in his bones, and Morgan lifted me and threw me overhead, using my weight against me, and I fell to the hard sand.

I lay on the ground, Morgan above me. Blood poured from the wound in his shoulder. He stared at me, and took my stone blade in his hand, and yanked it out of his flesh, and threw it away, out into the darkness.

"More," he said, and charged at me as I scrambled to my feet, his eyes filled with fire. He smiled now, not wavering, a constant grin, as he grabbed me with his heavy hands, trying to throttle me. I punched him in the stomach, over and over, hitting him with all my might, and he grunted with each strike. He squeezed my throat, and I struggled to breathe.

"You are stronger, pup, but not enough," he said, and did his best to crush my windpipe. My fingers reached to the wound in his shoulder, and then dug, sliding into the cut and ripping at his flesh. He yelled in pain and let go, and I was on top of him, and with one hand in his gashed shoulder, I punched with the other, raining down blows to his face. His nose finally snapped, and I smiled. My nose had healed crooked, and I would give him the same misery.

Morgan grinned a bloody smile and grabbed my wrist and squeezed. He was still stronger than me, even with my advantage, and he flipped us over, on top now, and closed his hands around my throat. His face filled my vision, his bloodstained grin all I saw. He strangled me, his hands squeezing tight.

"You have failed, pup," he said. "You were not enough. You will never reach her."

I couldn't breathe, spots in my vision, and I reached, reached for anything, and my hands touched something hard, and hot, and it burned, but I held it anyway, and swung it around, pressing the emberous wood into Morgan's face, pressing it into his open eyes.

He didn't shout now, but screamed, as the heat seared his eyes, and he rolled away, holding them, hoping to will his sight back. His legs kicked, the pain too much to bear.

I breathed again, my vision clear, and I stood. Morgan rolled on the ground, screaming.

My hands burned, the flesh peeling. The piece of hardwood was nearby, and I grabbed it again, wincing at the heat. I would only need it for a short time.

I swung it down hard onto Morgan's head, with a heavy thud, and he grunted, his hands shielding him, and I brought it down again, and again, until his arms were limp. I swung until I heard his skull crack, and his breathing stop.

43

I do not know when it is.

I have lost track of time. After killing Morgan, I—

What did I do?

I left him. I left his body on the sandy plains, and I continued back into the hallways, back into the maze.

Yes, I returned to the maze and listened once again to the compass. The Lover was dead, my last obstacle to you, and without him in the way, the compass would lead me back. Between it, and my new knowledge of the Thirteen, I would find you again, and pull you from this prison.

And so I searched. I walked every step of hallways, exhaustively criss-crossing worlds, my feet hardening with every step, my legs granite, my body steel. The dark organ in me still kicked, but it waited, humming, deep in my belly.

Alas, the compass, it did nothing. My chest held it silently, my heart beating, my lungs breathing, but it did not quake. It sang no song, no matter where I stepped, no matter which door I approached.

Had coming so close to you exhausted it? Despite its intimate attachment to me, I knew nothing about its workings. It was Suffolk's work, his solution to finding you. Still, it may yet kick on, and sing its song once again.

I must be patient.

But so I have delved, patiently, waiting to see you again.

The worlds blend, and with the Thirteen, I avoid the dangers, earmarked by constellations, the worlds of plague, of ravage, of death and destruction.

Hunger is still my constant companion, but I survive. I forage, I scavenge, and I eat from the land. It is not always pleasant, often not, I must admit, but I know each meal that sustains me, regardless of its content, brings me closer to you.

But I do not find you, and my heart yearns. After the rage of hunting Morgan, of tracking the vagrant rogue that abated your imprisonment, of the ceaseless anger I held for so long, now I am empty, filled only with sadness, and the strong urge for the gentle touch of your powerful heart. Twice now it has been taken from me, just as I would caress you, and twice now it has broken me.

I search endlessly for you, hoping to turn a corner, to emerge from a door, and there you will be, and this time there will be no Morgan, no shifting maze. I will find you alone, and alone I will find you, and then rescue you.

They told me it was a fool's errand, they did, so long ago. My parents, they told me I was squandering their money, wasting my time studying superstition. Father, oh Father. The rage in his eyes when I said I had bought the House. And Mother. She only wanted me to marry, to settle, to find a career.

They didn't understand, couldn't understand. For I had you. I found your calls, your pleas for help, and who was I but to answer? The noble knight, lost in our time, must change shape.

And I have gone through so much on this lofty quest. I struggle to recognize the man I have become when I see my reflection in a pool of water.

Where are you, Beloved?

Still, I search. I have bedded for the night, sleeping on the soft moss of a fairy forest, one of the more pleasant worlds, having steered clear of the venomous fae that live somewhere in the wood. I am sheltered here, but I must leave it, like I leave every world. They are temporary, transient, connected to this maze, to the hallways. To your prison.

The mystery of its construction eludes me. I have solved many riddles in my delving, but the nature of it is still clouded. The Architect is innocent, proven by the young Suffolk. I trust his words. Then who did it? My research brought up other names in connection, but I did not find them responsible. Ayad? Clarence?

I don't think so. This is beyond human hands. Only given human shape, with hallways and doors.

I thought it one of your rivals, I have, as I have wandered since the death of Morgan, my mind once again open to the wondering. But that is not in their nature. They would not wage war like this, surely not. It would be an insidious torment, without the hope of rescue. This is against their creed.

Then what is left?

I do not know. And perhaps I may not know. In the end, if I succeed in my rescue, in my hope, I would gladly trade an eternal mystery of this maze. With you out of it, it will stay dormant forever, below the thousand steps, below the House above, below Plainmoor. I will have it walled, never to be seen again by human eyes.

I sleep now, Beloved. I need the rest. I dream of finding you on the morrow, the morrow I cannot measure.

44

It has been so long. I still cannot find you.

I have seen them skulking about, Beloved.

I mentioned them before to you, and I let them be, let them delve deeper. Let them discover the dark secrets of the hallways on their own, and see if they can divine the mysteries of the Thirteen, as they jump through doors, hoping their faith can lead them to you.

But I was foolish.

Foolish to think they could hunt and peck inside the maze, searching for your heart, sharing the same mission as me, foolish to think they could be left alone, left to their own devices.

For was that not what the Lover was? He was once like them, skulking, rapacious, scoundrels. Morgan had been like them, a simple explorer, and then he transformed over time, the maze and the search turning him into a monster, a traitor to you.

Any of them could become the Lover. Perhaps even they are. Suffolk's words of cycles still echo. One of the young miscreants could be Morgan, could be a young Lover, and if I cut them off at the root now, they will never blossom into an accomplice warden, keeping you imprisoned.

It is for the best.

The first had set up camp on the wooden floorboards, in a corner meeting of two hallways. He carried a pack of sorts, of a making I could not recognize. Indeed, his garb was strange, but I dismissed it. Immaterial details. He was a man, and he was a danger.

I greeted him as a friend, raising my arms in peace, calling out to him. He looked at me with confusion at first. I make a strange impression, I know, with my current appearance, with the amalgamation of clothing I wear, and my bloated torso, and my swollen nose. I can even appear the monster.

But when he saw I came in peace, he smiled, and beckoned me to join him. He raised to shake my hand. I took his hand and pulled him in.

I drew my blade, and stabbed him a dozen times, his face turning grim as I slid the dagger into him, over and over, cutting through the tenuous bindings that connected him to life. He slumped over in my arms, and I let him fall.

I took a cursory glance at his belongings and took some of his rations, eating as I looked. There was a journal, some belongings. Wasteful. I left them behind, along with his pack and his supplies.

I did not leave his body.

I carried it, his blood leaking out onto my outclothes. His weight burdened me, but I was strong, hardened by my time, and I made do. I would need a place for them.

I passed by rooms, waiting for a call from the Thirteen. And then I saw the room, and went inside, and placed his body. I laid it carefully. I smiled, knowing my work was not done.

The second was traversing the snail world, as I have taken to call it. I called out to him, letting him believe he was safe. That I was another taken traveler, and I would help him.

The third fought back, a wily man, who knew how to fight, his fists quick to clench, and raise, a boxer. But he had no weapon, and I endured the blows until his fists gave out.

The fourth never saw me. He slept on the wooden floors. His sandy hair was mussed, his face at peace. It did not belie the potential inside him. He could be the next one to stop me, to tackle me on the precipice of greatness, on the verge of touch.

I slit his throat.

The fifth knew me.

"Henry!" he called out, and he smiled. It slowed me as I approached.

How did he know me? I did not recognize him, a brutish face, with a simple haircut. His clothes were plain, but well tailored. He was amply supplied, in his camp in the hallways.

"You have my name. What is yours?" I asked.

"Thompson," he said. "Like the gun." He stood. "May I shake your hand?"

"You are not armed, are you?"

"I carry a short knife, aye," he said. "But I mean no harm."

I eyed him. Any deception he carried was well stowed. I meant to end him, but my curiosity stayed my hand. I approached, ready for an attack, but one didn't come. He shook my hand and held it with warmth.

"How do you know me?"

"You led me here," he said. "My studies brought me to your name. And then to the House above."

"You came through the House?" I asked. "How? I locked it tight."

He eyed me. "They thought you dead, up above. I bought the deed."

"You what?" I asked. He put out a wary hand, holding me back.

"I have no ill will. Ownership of the thing is not important. I suspected you still lived. And here you are. Have you found Suffolk?"

I glared at him, at his curious eyes, and I did not wait, and swiped out with my blade, in a motion he could not track, and his throat opened. He stared back incredulously. He could not believe his fate.

Seldom few did.

The sixth was a mercy. He was raving, a madman, his skin burnt, his body parched, come stumbling in from the desert. I killed him quickly, a blessing to him.

I stacked him with the others. All six, laid neatly.

Cycles, indeed.

No more interlopers, Beloved. Now, the path is clear. You will be mine. Mine alone.

45

Where are you, Beloved?

I have searched, searched, and come up empty. The compass, it sings no more, and I question if it will ever sing again. The metal instrument, embedded, has gone dormant. I tap on it, touch it, hoping I can will it back to life, but it stays dead.

Where are you?

The hallways are deserted, now. I prowl them alone, silently, but I hear nothing. Not the echoing footfalls of the Hounds. Not the steps of Morgan or Suffolk, or any of the young strangers that come in our wake.

Thompson, his name was. He owned the House above, he said. When is it, up above? How many years have passed in my time down here? How old am I, truly?

I pass by, and see my reflection, and I scarcely recognize the man I have become. I tell myself it does not matter, that my appearance is ephemeral, but I cannot help but think of myself as a youth, when I entered, when I took the thousand steps for the first time. It was a different life, a man I cannot discern.

I have crossed a thousand worlds, I am sure of it, but none have brought me closer to your heart. I know it is here, somewhere in the hallways, and I hope every corner turned brings me within sight of it, and I will sprint toward you, I will embrace your heart, and I will carry it out, back through those one thousand worlds, up those one thousand steps, and out of the House, back into whatever time the world has passed.

I search, my weary feet crossing wooden floorboards, over and over, stamping onto them, the same boards, and I know this place now, I know the Thirteen, and the doors to use and which to avoid, know the thousand thousand worlds, the infinite worlds, some of which are mine and some of which are not, but—

But I do not know it.

I cannot, simple proof positive, where if I knew this place, I would know you. I would find your holy heart and bring it to salvation. So after all the pain and horror, the damage inflicted on me and onto others, my hands now killers, I am still empty-handed.

It leaves a void inside me.

The dark godflesh organ is my only companion. It pulses and shakes, kicking at its womb, but it does not threaten birth. I once worried it would rip me apart from within, but I now know it is incapable of such a thing. If it is to be born, I must be the midwife.

And to tell the truth, its movement is my only solace. I do not know its language, and why it sometimes moves, but it is still a comfort.

A small comfort.

The void inside me grows. It is a dark and harrowing thing, a feeling that I know the name, but which I hesitate to give voice. I dare not speak it, or send it to you, because it is an admittance. A feeling that has tugged at the corners of my heart for a long time, but one I have ignored, have pushed away, have hidden deep inside my heart.

Doubt.

I say it aloud, and tears form, and I cry, sobbing, my heart weeping for the accrued loss of endless time. For the hard wooden floors and walls, for the thousand thousand worlds.

My missives have come less and less frequent, yes, because I have been using my time to search for you. Yes, that is a truth.

But also because you are not listening. You have not been listening. A hundred heartfelt pleas, of a story told, searching for your heart, begging for help, earnest dedications. All have fallen on deaf ears.

So why do I speak? Why do I send to you? Why?

I do not think I will find you, Beloved. I have searched fruitlessly, sacrificed everything I am and could be, and I am no closer to you than I ever was. No closer to you than the moment I entered the maze. You are beyond my reach or grasp.

Where am I?

I do not know.

47

I have found my way back to the beginning.

I recognize this hallway. So long ago, when I thought a straight line would lead me to you. When I thought this was simple.

I have wandered long in my doubt, Beloved. I explored deeply, delving deep into the maze. I crossed through every world.

And despite it all, I searched for you.

I didn't intend to, but my eyes still scanned for your heart. At the end of every hallway, at every corner turned.

I did not find you.

I wandered. I survived. I traveled across many worlds and saw many things. As a young man, my head in books, studying, researching, I would have killed for time in these places. I would want all the knowledge contained within. I would need to answer every mystery, to pursue every crumb of question and devour them, and note it to the letter with paper and pen.

But instead I wandered. I sat in the mushroom forest, stared down into the void over the bridge of light, and wandered the hallways all the same.

I feel old, and the wrinkles cut across my face agree. The passage of time is undeniable, despite that I cannot track it. Or perhaps it tracks faster here. I do not know, but I cannot argue with the ache in my bones or the creases in my skin.

I find myself back at the beginning. A few rooms, and a few choices, lay between me and the thousand stairs that lead back to the surface. I intend to leave.

What waits for me on the surface, I do not know. I worry my parents have died with the great passage of time. In fact, I worry the world has passed me by. My life is this cage, this prison. Here, I am able. Here, I am skilled.

But knowledge of the Thirteen will not serve me in the world. The godflesh grown will be nothing but a tumorous excision. It will not provide me warmth in a normal home. It's suckling kicks will do nothing but target it for removal.

But I have pushed those fears aside. All of them are minuscule compared to the doubt, the emptiness, the sorrow. They are too large to ignore. And I may not get another chance to escape.

I embark on my last journey, my way out. After I leave the hallways, we will not speak again.

48

Through all my time here, I had not forgotten the horror of swimming through the lake of gore, in the cavern of flesh.

It stayed with me, like any of my journeys. I could not forget it, and neither could I think of a fate worse.

I knew the thousand stairs were through this door, but the anxious fear returned, the hesitation I had felt only long ago. I knew the Thirteen now, and this door was marked as dangerous. As poison. I never would open this door, not unless there was no other choice.

But this was the way out. And so I opened the door. It closed behind me, now no longer a door, the wooden door transforming.

I had thought there was little worse than the cavern of flesh, of being inside some massive organ, as it processed corpses, feeding the pit of death, the lake of blood.

I was wrong, for when I had entered the room the first and only time, it had been living. It had been pink, and vital, and alive.

Now it rotted.

The once vital floorflesh had grown a sickly hue, turning yellow brown. The flesh tore under my feet, unable to bear my weight, and I sunk knee deep into the rotten tissue.

Worse still was the smell. I was surrounded by rot, by sulfurous death, and I coughed, coughed, tearing a scrap piece of cloth, and forcing it in front of my nose and mouth before I vomited. I retched, dry heaving, the odor vile.

The corpses inside the massive cavern had long since rotted, and no more had piled in. The cavern itself was the source of the smell.

I had to make it through. I knew the way. I only had to make it there, to the other side of the lake, to the other sphincterous door, and emerge.

I carried no pack, no supplies. I had to only cross this terrible lake.

But it was a lake no more. The lake had been filled with blood, a crimson pond, teeming with viscera. As the cavern had rotted, the blood had dried, coagulating. Now it was muddy marsh, a murky stinking coagulation, and my feet sunk into it, unleashing an even more awful smell, and I could not hold the fabric over my face, needing both my hands to balance myself as I trudged through the gory mire.

I sunk deeper with each step, the blood turning into quicksand, a thick muck that would swallow me whole. With every step, I pushed down, and sunk further, first to my hips, and then to stomach, and above, and I would drown here, suffocate in this horror—

I stopped, slowing myself down. I scurried to the surface of the blood-swamp, and let my weight spread out along as much of my body as possible. If I must crawl, so be it.

I moved like a snake through the gore, my body covered in the thick, viscous, rotten hell. I stopped to retch, throwing up what little water I held in my stomach, followed by bile. It mattered little. There was nothing that could make the smell worse.

I crawled, knee after elbow, a hundred yards of putrid blood, and then onto the far shore, past the stacks of corpses, through the rotted cavern.

I forced myself up to my feet, my knees and hips aching, shaking off all the gore, like a wet dog, pushing it off me back onto the fragile, disgusting groundmeat.

I walked, stepping light, even as my feet tore through the flesh of this massive organ, dead now, rotting. The smell was horrendous, but I still breathed, forcing the air in and out, so I would not asphyxiate, even as it singed my lungs. I stepped across the rotten cavern, and I saw the other door, what was left of it, and I opened it, stepping through, back into the hallways.

49

To escape, I must pay. I knew I would. It did not make the payment easier.

A scale sat on the table, with a knife. The scale shone dully, brass. It was empty, one arm on the table, the other in the air.

The knife sat next to it, simple, clean, and sharp as a razor.

I had passed through this room many years ago, and had given it dried meat, a portion of sausage, and it had taken it as adequate payment. A way to balance the scales.

But I carried no food on me, not anymore. I had reasoned so long ago, that any delver could pass through the room easily, provided they were willing to part with a toe, or a finger.

A pound of flesh, to balance the scales. To pay the proper amount.

I did not measure the amount of meat I left before, but perhaps I should have. So I would not cut more than necessary.

It was a simple thought. The way out lay through this room, past this scale. I simply needed to pay the price.

Simple, but not easy. Which of my remaining fingers would I sacrifice? My essential right? Or should I cut from my left? Or perhaps a handful of toes. Which would I want more, when I returned to the surface? I seldom think of my toes, but I use them every day.

The sweat beaded on my forehead, and wiped at it, a film of gory grime coming off with it. I could clean myself on the surface. All the clean water in the world, within easy reach.

I grabbed the knife and studied its edge. It was sharp, sharper than the stone I still carried.

I walked to an empty spot on the table and laid my left hand down. I took a deep breath.

I was leaving this place, and this was as much proof as any.

I forced the knife down on the top knuckle of my left pinkie. The blade sliced quickly through the muscle and flesh, but caught on my bone, and I pressed down with my weight, and it cut through the point. I gritted my teeth, the pain filling me. I put the piece of flesh on the scale, and it did not budge.

Blood spurted from my finger, and stopping now would not help. I cut again, slicing through another knuckle, carving it away, and I added it to the scale. Still no movement.

I would have sworn the meat I added on the way in was as much as that, a slight amount. But then I realized.

There was no reason the price would always be the same. And of course, it would cost more to leave than to enter.

Pain screamed at me from my hand, but I continued, slicing off the rest of my pinkie, and then continuing with the ring finger of my left hand.

It was more difficult, thicker, but I bared down the blade and it cut through the bone at the top knuckle, and agony flared through me again. Dark blood poured onto the table from my fingers, but I did not stop. I couldn't stop, couldn't pay this much without paying it all.

I would escape this place.

I placed it on the scale. Still no movement, and a dark anxiety rose in me, alongside frustration and fury, and I cut through another knuckle, and placed it, and no change of the scale, and I cut through the last knuckle, the bone snapping as I forced the blade through, blood pouring from my hand now. I placed the last of the finger on the scale, now two full fingers, and it moved.

How much more would I pay?

Two fingers and a thumb remaining on my left hand.

I could sacrifice the pinkie on my right.

I switched the knife to my left hand, awkward with fewer fingers, but I did not require precision. Only force.

I took another halting breath, and placed the blade at the base of my pinkie finger. All at once. All at once.

I sliced hard, pressing my weight into it, and it snapped through the bone, and I gasped, blood spurting from the hole.

I placed it on the scale. Still not enough.

How much more would I pay?

I took off my shoes.

I made the same bargain with my feet. I would carve off the two small toes of each foot, if it required it. But I would not take the others. I would need them if I were to escape. I would find the flesh elsewhere.

I started with my left foot. The arm moved slightly with each added toe. It wavered with the two small toes from my right foot. Blood spurted from my feet now, and a deep pain shot up my legs. I would stop the bleeding after I was done. After I was out of this cursed room.

The scale was almost balanced. It would require only a little more.

I took my left ear in my grasp and pulled it, leaving an entry point for the knife. I could not see my work, but the knife worked easily through the soft flesh of my ear, and I gritted my teeth as I finished, prying the tissue away from my head.

I put the ear down on the scale, no longer mine, and it balanced, finally. I escaped the room, the opposite door unlocked, hurrying, before the cost rose.

50

I eventually stopped the bleeding.
    I walked the beach, once again.
    I emerged on the other side.
    I—
    I walked the beach, once again.
    Charlie was gone. All that remained was destruction.
    I went through the door, and it vanished behind me. I had to move forward, and so I did. I walked the beach, the sand laid out in front of me. I tread the same path I had so long ago. The wind whipped past, the vast ocean spread before me, the waves frothing as they topped out above my head, crashing down. Behind the dunes soared, mirroring the dark water.
    There was nothing else. The water, the sand, the dunes. The allbeach persisted.
    But I looked down the beach, and waited, and there was no glint, no spark, no silvery light that caught my eye. How long had it been here, in this place? Had time passed at all? Was Charlie's progress the only marker of time on the allbeach? Was my progress the only marker of time in the hallways?
    I walked down the beach, my wounded feet aching, a thin trickle of blood occasionally staining the sand. I thought to stick them in the salt

water, to stem the blood, and to clean the wounds. But I remembered Charlie's words from long ago. To stay out of the water.

I continued walking to where Charlie had been. The stalwart fisherman, who served as many men.

He was gone, and all that remained was the legacy of a great catch.

Charlie had landed something, something big, had caught something larger than him, than me, than any man. The impression in the sand was enormous, almost too large to see across, and I stepped down into the crater, where whatever Charlie had caught had settled on the beach.

Its weight was incalculable, its size more than anything alive or dead, greater than the deepest whale. The sand had been compressed, in a massive divot. The incoming and outgoing tide had erased some of it, but it encompassed the entire beach.

I walked down into it, and stood in the middle of the colossal hole, and looked up to the dune, the towering dune, ten feet over my head. It had towered. But the catch, whatever Charlie had landed, had been dragged over the dune, the wall of sand now gone, pushed aside. The body had been taken, pulled, moved somehow, over the dunes.

I walked to the edge of the path, and I looked, peered at the trail.

I saw only dunes, and the trail of the massive weight, and nothing else.

The dim sky overhead stayed constant, and the waves crashed behind me.

Charlie had landed his catch. And now he dragged it home.

At least that's what I told myself. The fisherman had succeeded. He had caught What Dwelled Beneath the Waves. He had dragged it ashore.

I had the thought to follow. To follow in the wake of this vast beast, of the great catch, and see where the fisherman had taken it. To see the end of it, if it truly was that.

But the stairs lay ahead. That was the end of my story. The end.

So I walked out of the great crater, and down the beach, the massive ocean on one side, the endless dunes on the other, the allbeach, infinite in all directions, sand and water. I walked it until I encountered the second door.

Always a second door.

I opened it, a melancholic joy bursting in my heart. I would see the surface again. I would feel the true sun once more. I would sleep in a bed and have my wounds cared for. As I stepped through, I let those feelings-capture me. Not the earnest sadness of abandoning you. Not the desperate disappointment and frustration of failure, of quitting a mission that has taken uncountable time.

I let the joy capture me, for the sadness would stay long past.

But I emerged on the other side, expecting to face a thousand stairs, arcing up out of sight. The thousand stairs leading back to the House, to a time I may not know.

But the stairs were gone.

51

I have sat, staring at the blank wall. I have waited, waited, and still there is no change. The stairs are not there.

The maze, the hallways—they have always led from here, the origin. Why would it change now? Why would it be any different? This prison, this cage, it has always controlled me, has always shown its command.

I am a fool, a fool. Every time I believe I have an answer, the maze provides another question.

I got up, and I wandered. Back the way I came, perhaps the stairs have shifted. I wandered, back toward where they once had shifted, long ago.

I was done! I was through with this game, this quest, this mission! I have explored for years! For time beyond years, time I have not measured!

My body is broken, my face a wreck! The man I once was is long extinguished, ridden into a lake of viscera, stomped through an inferno, and lashed to a stone table! I have seen a thousand worlds, and my body teared and shifted as this maze has corrupted it! I have consumed the godflesh, and provided a home for a new organ inside me, have lost fingers and toes, have maimed and killed the innocent and guilty alike, to be the one that finds you!

I have walked ten thousand miles of wooden floorboards and learned the language of the Thirteen! I have stolen the Architect's compass and used its mechanical song to find you! Twice, twice, I nearly felt your caress, and both times it was stolen from me!

I had severed ties with my faith! It was impossible, impossible for me to lose you, but I did it anyway, and made my way to escape, because there was no other option! But now there are no stairs, there is no escape, because I have been the prisoner all along!

Wait.

I hear something.

52

I had forgotten. Of all the things, I had forgotten.

Cycles. Suffolk spoke of them, and then became a victim of them. I should have known, should have realized.

But it had been so long. I had forgotten. And I have paid for my failure of memory. Another failure.

I heard a scattering of footsteps echoing toward me. The sound of boots on hardwood, and I thought it impossible, but realized it was not. Just because I had cleared the hallways of any other delvers, did not mean they would stop. There was no end of knights, all pursuing the improbable quest.

I waited, poised, ready, and then got up, waiting for more steps. I heard none and took that as a moment to retreat. I wanted no encounter, not in my current state. I hurried, my clumsy feet disobeying me, still learning to walk with ravaged toes.

I moved as fast as I could, but torture shot up my legs. I rushed, and then heard the steps behind me again, faster now, and I ran again, and the man behind me yelled after me.

I turned, and I saw him.

I saw what I once was.

An unblemished, innocent face. One that had yet to face real hardship, had yet seen his faith tested. A face unbroken, and form unblemished. The sight hurt my heart. I could not face it, could not face the man I once was.

I ran as fast as I could, as hard as my legs would allow. The blood flowed from my wounded feet again, and the maze vibrated beneath me, and I remembered.

I ran, ran, hoping to avoid history. I would break the continuity of this cycle, I would this time.

My footsteps were still behind me, and I ran, ran as the floor shifted.

I heard him yelling, and I turned, and then a shot rang out, and he was gone, the maze turned.

The pain in my toes, my hands, my ear, they had disappeared, replaced by a burning in my side.

Panic raised in my mind, alarm for my godflesh, but no, the bullet had hit my other side, two inches in, burrowing a hole in me, and not escaping.

Agony flares through me, Beloved.

Please, help me.

53

This bullet will kill me.

I cannot extract it, not without accelerating my decline. It is in me, having carved an inexorable path through my guts. I can feel myself bleeding inside, and I will die.

Of all the things present in this prison, a mundane bullet will be my end. The blood leaks from the wound. I let it. I will not see the sun again.

I want to lie here and let death take me. It is the only other escape available. The thought has always stayed with me, in the back of my mind. Death has always been there, a loyal companion, ready to claim me. I have escaped it many times.

It has been victorious in the end. Death and the hallways, after all my adaptation, after I have become a whetted and honed blade, it did not matter. A simple bullet fired from the past was enough to stop me.

But if it will be the end of me, I will go out as I came in.

I force myself to sit up, propping myself up against the wooden wall, the familiar wooden wall, a color and hue I could match in blindness.

I reach for the compass, the metal embedded in my chest, that once led me to you. It is has not sung since that day, no thrumming, no song, no sign of life. I pondered about why, as I wandered. Had such closeness to you overwhelmed its mechanical nature? Had it simply reached the end of its lifespan as a construct? Had my blood broken it, a machine designed for the body of Suffolk?

I do not know. But I would rid myself of it, before I died.

I took a grip of it, the slick metal, and pulled, pulled with all my might. But it did not move. My flesh tugged with it, the compass firmly implanted in me. I pulled harder again. I would pull it out, I would pull it out, but it resisted once again, and it was clear I did not have the strength.

So be it.

I found my knife, my stone knife, which had served me well, and had tasted blood. It would taste mine, finally.

I inserted the edge of the blade around the outer rim of the compass, the circular metal piece, and pressed down, pain ripping through me. It threatened to knock me unconscious, but I focused, breathing. I had endured so much. This would not be the end of me, and I pressed harder still, the sharp edge of the knife cutting through my tender flesh. I slid it deeper, until I felt the edge of the compass, and then I sliced around, sawing away at the flesh held tight to the gripping metal hooks of the device. I yelled out in agony, but I stayed awake, and forced the stone knife all the way around. I pulled out the blade, setting it aside.

I set my three fingers around the edge of the metal and I pulled again, and this time, the compass moved, and I yanked harder, tugging with all might, and then it finally let go, ripping from my flesh, and I screamed one last time, and then pulled it out, dropping the heavy piece of metal with a clunk. It sat there, pieces of flesh still clinging to it, my blood staining the floor.

My fingers probed the edges of the hole it left in me. It was a gory mess, but it seemed smaller now, now that the compass was gone. I breathed hard. Blood seeped from the wound, as well as from my gunshot. I ached, the wound singing.

I sat there, waiting. How long would I last here? How long until I lost too much blood? Would time here keep me alive forever, slow my death down to a crawl?

Then I felt it. The gentle kicking, the movement.

The godflesh. It had slept, dormant for quite some time. It kicked again, and then again, harder. My hand went to the bulbous growth on my side, and the organ pushed, pressing at my skin.

"I'm sorry, young one," I said. "Perhaps you will be born in my grave."

But it did not stop. Instead, it moved more, pushing, pushing.

Had removing the compass awoken it? Was the mechanical means anathema to it?

It pushed again, the same way, and a question arose in my mind, and despite my pain, despite the agony, I forced myself to my feet, and walked toward its prodding. I drove my legs forward in the hallway, until I came to a choice, a left or right, and the godflesh kicked to the left.

I trudged on battered feet, missing toes, until I came to another, a choice of straight or right, and the growing darkness in me nudged me to the right, and I followed.

It moved me, pushed me. The god-organ would lead me, and in my dying days, I would follow.

54

The godchild led me.
    I did not know where I would go, but I went as fast as condition would allow.
    Where was I going? Where was this nascent flesh taking me? Would I venture to dream again?
    But I cannot help the impulse, the daring dream that perhaps the organ, the thing, the child, whatever it may be, was not leading me to a random, arbitrary place.
    Would I allow myself the hope, the hope it was leading me to you?
    The compass had been my companion for many ages down in the hallways, and had served me, bringing me to you, before the Lover stalled my success.
    But had I wandered fruitlessly? Had I searched endlessly, without progress, because I had clung to the fruits of another's labor? Because I had trusted the hope of another, of Suffolk, the broken man, who had returned to the maze after years away, after the Hounds had made their mark?
    He had not searched for you out of faith, or joy, or love. He had searched for you, hoping you could end the pursuit of the Hounds. Or perhaps for revenge, for the loss of his child and wife. But he had come back with anger and control in mind, and had devised mechanical means to find you. It

had been fruitless, both for him, and for me.

Had I been a fool for far too long? Trusting in a failed means, when the way had been growing inside me all this time? The godflesh—the Scientist, who fertilized its growth—had I gone through those doors not through happenstance?

I could not know, and I still walked down endless hallways, the wooden floors tormenting my severed toes, blood leaking from my chest and side, staining the wood behind me.

But the god-organ led me still, pushing me through, and I followed, without food, without water, losing blood. I was not infinite, no matter how much I had adapted to this place, and if the path continued on forever, I would soon die on my feet.

I followed the urging of the organ. It pressed against my skin, moving, pushing. Not just against my skin, but against my innards, against my intestines and kidney and muscle and fibrous tissue, and I realized this was separate from its leading.

For it was leading, yes, urging me onward at every junction, but it was also growing.

It had grown in me, once, especially after the implantation of the smooth pink stone, the work of the Scientist, who I had bled in his workshop. The smooth pink stone, that I thought of as a piece of the godflesh now, after all this time.

But it had grown, become bulbous, stretching my skin, distending my abdomen, a growth I had learned and owned as part of myself, the piece of flesh I consumed spurring the enlargement, and the pink stone spurring even more. And indeed, there was a time I worried the new organ would grow too large, and burst through my skin, and I would die here for my once hunger for the harvested piece of oily godsteak.

But it had stopped. It had gone dormant, only occasionally waking to remind me of its presence, and then sleeping once more.

But now, now it grew, and grew quickly, pressing outward on my skin, and inside, toward my guts, but I still followed. If it would grow, and kill me, let it do it now, as my time waned.

I followed the urging of the organ. I would do it as it led me, if it would lead me to substance.

If it would lead me to you.

Down hallway after hallway, turning, I did not mark my progress, did not mark my trail, for I would not be returning. I went wildly, flesh commanding me forward, and I followed.

I walked, walked, my feet wet with blood, my body slick with crimson and sweat, and I walked, my whole body agony, the organ growing inside me, pressing me tight inside, but I walked, I walked.

I passed a hundred doors, a hundred more, the constellation of Thirteen on all of them, and I read them, none of them leading them to you. They all were calamity, all pain, all distraction.

I walked, I walked, and then the godflesh stopped me, pulling me toward the door, and I looked at its engraving, at the constellation, and the sudden hope I had kept quiet inside surged to the surface, my heart and hope bursting.

The Thirteen.

In all my time in the hallways, I seldom had seen a constellation with over ten lit. It was a rarity to see eleven, and I had seen twelve lit stars fewer times than the fingers on my hands.

But never all Thirteen.

The Crone, The Dweller, The All, The None. The Beast, The King and Queen. The Weapon, The Forge. The Darkness and Light. The Insects. The Shape, The Shadow. And you, Beloved.

All Thirteen lights shone there, above this door. The door was not special, as none of the doors were special, another door, with a twin, somewhere deep within its bounds.

The godflesh had led me here, here at the end.

I opened it, and stepped through.

55

I was wrong, Beloved.

This door is special.

It is the door of all doors.

I went through, the growing godchild pushing me forward, the growth inside searching with me.

Always two doors, is what the fisherman said, so long ago. And he'd been proven right, time after time.

But not today, not in this room. This room had fourteen doors. The one through which I entered, and the thirteen that sat opposite it, in the dark void.

The void was complete, outside of the doors, soft, unearthly, emerald light around them, but nothing else. No distance, no horizon, no sun, no moon. Only the doors.

I have seen many doors, and many rooms in my time here, Beloved. I have not seen them all, for I have not enough heartbeats, but I have seen many, a great swathe of many worlds, awful and beautiful, enormous and minuscule, alien and familiar.

But I have never seen this room before. All thirteen lights, leading to thirteen doors.

The Thirteen, of which you are one.

The emblems stand above the doors.
The Crone.
The Dweller.
The All.
The None.
The Beast.
The King and Queen.
The Weapon.
The Forge.
The Darkness and Light.
The Insects.
The Shape.
The Shadow.
And you, Beloved.

The blood runs down my side, leaking from the wound. I fear there is a sizable amount pooling inside me. I feel the inside of me, the push and pull of the child, but also the wrongness. The metal of the bullet, splintered, a deep pain that will not end until I die.

The blood disappears as it hits the void. Only nothingness below me, a dark emptiness that supports me, as I stare at the thirteen doors.

I walk to your door, the last, the thirteenth door, and I stand before it, staring up at your sign. No points of light, no constellation, not here. The doors only show the signs of the Thirteen.

Is it that simple? If I walk through this door, will you be there? Will your errant heart be waiting on the other side? The altar, which I have seen, but never touched, in front of me, once again?

But I hesitate, my hand hovering at the simple door knob, which matches every innumerable door. It flutters, there, shaking. From the pain, from the blood, missing precious fingers.

I look to the other doors. Each marked by one of the Thirteen. Were they here as well? Was there a piece of each of them down here, down in the labyrinth, waiting for a delver?

I had no sense of them, no pull, no trace, but—

But perhaps I had been foolish. Perhaps, since the very beginning. I had focused too much on my singular quest. Thinking myself special, thinking myself unique.

But time has proven me wrong. I am one of many, of the many who've come down here, through time and space, searching for the key to you, your immortal heart.

But twice now, I've rushed to your heart, within quick sight, and then it has been taken from me. Both leading to disaster. Both leading to death. Both leading to change.

And now, here, I stand at the precipice. The thing inside me, that has grown, that kicks at the in of me—it wants you. It wants your heart, as I want your heart.

And as I weaken, as my blood drains from me, I think of what I've achieved down here. Of my parents, calling me a fool for following this quest. For searching for you.

It has cost me greatly.

Has it been worth the cost?

Has it been worth the cost?

The godchild pushes hard now, and my legs weaken below me. The gut shot will kill me soon.

I think to open another door. To peek through. To satisfy a final curiosity.

But I don't.

I stare out, into the great void, and then push through your door.

56

Beloved, where are you

There is no space again, only visions, overwhelming information, pressing data, the pain in my gut, my chest, my fingers, my toes, the blood pouring from me and pooling in me gone, too much knowledge, flooding my eyes.

I see everything, all at once, and tears pour from me, my mind unable to perceive it.

Again, I remember, I remember back, an eternity ago, the room of steam and data, of bombs and visions of the future. I am there again, but no, it is different this time.

But then pieces pull through, overwhelming. Pieces I recognize, one by one.

You.

I see you, your form, dominant, towering over the landscape, as you march across the land, leading an army. An army of lovers, all betrothed to you, and I am among them.

And I am truly not alone, one of many, one of millions, The Beloved, the inspirer, the one of love and faith, pulling us all forward, as we conquer every nation, one world under your awesome love.

I march, march, with no jealousy, no envy, my eyes staring only at your beautiful form, massive, powerful, impossible, magnificent.

You command us and we follow, holding your banner high, your symbol, the same as the Thirteenth door, the symbol of you and your power, and we carry it high, hold it above all, above everything on the Earth, above the past, the present, the future, over life and death, over the promise of family or career, your love all that matters, because you live now, your heart reclaimed, your body full, and you live and breathe, as only you live and breathe, and you walk.

But it is one of many things I see, for I see us march for you, but I also see you rule, see the success of our efforts, as we spread your love across the world.

Against fire and flame, against the belching of guns and radical storm of bombs unheard of, it doesn't matter, you are victorious, because there is no other path, not with you, Beloved, no, with your heart, with your heart that I have found, and returned, you are strong again, as I read a thousand times, your power, your love, full and formed, and you now reclaim all that was taken from you, by the creator of this horrible prison, but I have succeeded, and the Earth has been transformed.

It is for you, an altar to your beauty, to your strength, to the power of your form, and the impossibility of your existence. The billions amass around your resting place, waiting, hoping for a single glimpse of you, to praise you, to bow to you, to hope for a glance in their direction. They grovel, they beg, they starve as they wait, unable to leave to feed. If they die, it is as a martyr to their love to you, adoring forever.

And I still see you, at the end of all things, still there, dominant, all loving, as we strip the Earth with your love, all in service to you, monuments, altars, all to express the impossible devotion in our hearts to you, and yet we try.

It floods through me in a moment, my body forgotten, my mind reeling from the power of the vision, seeing all you accomplish, knowing the truest extent of my success.

I see it all, everything, from the beginning to the end, the true length of you, the full and absolute. I do not breathe, I do not hurt, I do not think, I only am, as the entirety flows through me.

And then I emerge, a moment passing, but the fullness in me, and I open my eyes, the pain full again, blood pouring from me, on my hands and knees.

I look up, and I see you, Beloved. You are there, only a scant few feet from me, perched on the altar.

Your glorious heart.

57

I see you, Beloved. My journey is nearly at an end.

Blood pours from my side now, amassing in me, but I sense the limit of it. I have only so much to give.

But not yet. I won't be thwarted again, not even by the limits of my body.

I have been here twice before, your glorious heart within view.

In this moment, the maze does not shift. It does not rumble, does not threaten to move, to push me away from you. To hide you. No. I have mastered it, and I have found my way here. It does not dare to move.

There is no Lover here. I bled him, killed him. Abandoned his body in a dark world. And then headed off any potential threats. He had said I wasn't ready. Said you had told him.

I proved him wrong, time and time again, as I navigated the maze, learned the lessons.

The stairs are ahead of me, and I push up them, toward your heart.

I crossed through a thousand worlds, met emissaries of the deep, saw the fragments of dead planets, and the births of new.

I fought through hell, through blood, through heat and cold, through starvation and suffering. All for you.

I fed upon gods.

I have seen the cycles, the start and end.

I am alone, now, with you, and it was all worthwhile, all for this moment.

The pain rips through me now, shuddering, staggering agony, and I fall, my body hitting the hard edges of the steps, but I don't feel it, the suffering too much. It is not the bullet wound, or the weeping hole in my chest from where I pulled the compass, but it is—

Pain, more misery, as something inside pushes and pulls, expanding, growing, the nascent god in me, nursing, suckling at me and the pink stone, for so, so long, now it grows, pushing at my skin, something inside me, agonizing pain

No, I cannot fail now, you are so close. Whatever is inside me, I must hold your heart. I must possess it before I go.

The blood sluices from me, cascading down the white stairs behind me, stark contrast, and I reach ahead of me, pulling myself up the steps.

I see your heart, enormous, black, the thing of legend, your purest soul, the last piece.

I climb, pulling myself, but the child pulls again at the inside of me, muscles tearing, organs stretching, bones cracking, and my spine snaps as the creature grows, and my legs are gone, no feeling, but I still have my arms, and I pull.

Stair by stair, my fingers reach for cold stone, and hard edge, and pull, and my body slides, the blood serving as oil for the climb.

So much blood

So much blood

How do I have so much

The child pushes at the bounds of me

No. I will touch you, Beloved. I will possess you. My first and deepest promise. I will be your salvation.

I climb, my hands my hooks, my meager fingers, all I have left to finish my journey.

The pain, it rips inside me, the flesh growing, something inside, the stranger, the child, my child, but I must have you first. I must have you first.

I climb, I climb, crawling up the steps, and you are close, and my skin rips, muscle and sinew tearing, no, not yet, and I tense, and hold myself together, keeping the godthing prisoner for a moment longer.

Just long enough.

Yours Forever

    I reach, and pull, the final step ahead of me, the altar above, and I am there. I am a creature of blood, everything I touch crimson, but I pull.

    Your heart is there, and I look, I cannot fathom, heavy, black, precarious, impossible, but true, my goal, my love, Beloved.

    I reach, I reach, my scant fingers grazing you, and then grasping you, electric in my hands, and I pull you from your altar, and I hold you.

    I hold you in my grasp. A dream. I squeeze you, I embrace you, your being, the deepest part of you, me, mine, us.

    And then the pain rips through me again, a harder tear, my skin pulling apart, and the agony is too much, but then it is replaced by nothing, the nerves ripped from my skin from within, the godthing emerging from me, as I lie at the base of your altar, holding you still, with deadened fingers. I see a shape emerge from me, a dark figure, covered in my viscera, my gore sloughing off its perfect form.

    I—

    You.

    You stand upright, pulling the fullness of your body from me, staggering, golden eyes staring down, your mouth open, and it is haggard, you still fight for life, and but then you see me, and what I hold.

    I should have known. I should have known, I was right, right all along. My destiny, my fate, our fate, interweaved. Cycles upon cycles, all leading here, all pulling me to this place, to you, carrying you, lover and mother.

    I've held you for years now, inside, nestled, and my heart rejoices, euphoria behind my eyes.

    You look down at me, at my bounty of your being, and you reach, and take your heart, and place it to your body, and envelop it once again.

    Born again, your heart yours, and you are whole, and you grow, you grow, and your mouth opens in a smile, and you bend to me, caressing my cheek with a dark finger.

    I stare up at you, as my last blood leaves, joyful.

    Yours forever.

Enjoy Yours Forever?

Sign up here to be notified about Robbie's next novel!

robbiedorman.com/newsletter

And don't forget to leave a review. Reviews are a direct way to help your favorite creators. We appreciate it.

Acknowledgements

Thank you to my wife Kim, for her patience and support, and my team of beta readers: Andrew, Carrie, Matt, Megan, and Yousef.

And thank you for reading.

About the Author

Robbie Dorman believes in horror. This Book is Cursed is his fifteenth novel. When not writing, he's podcasting, playing video games, or walking his dog. He lives in Florida with his wife, Kim.

You can follow Robbie on all social media @robbiedorman

His website is robbiedorman.com

Subscribe to his newsletter at robbiedorman.com/newsletter

Printed in the USA
CPSIA information can be obtained
at www.ICGtesting.com
CBHW031240090924
14023CB00021B/170/J